A Vow for the Vamp

Settle Myer

Contents

A Note from the Author

A Note from the Author

This book is a novella. It includes fated mates and in-staLUST. The characters fall fast and hard.

Included in this story are difficult topics of suicide (heavy), grief, controlling parents and emotional abuse by parents, death, killing, violence, blood/feeding, compulsion/controlling of female main character by deranged vamp, mention of SA (not by main character), mention of child vampires and deaths, mention of necrophilia, mention of forced and arranged marriage including that of a minor, mention of failed pregnancies, and terminal illness.

This book also includes cursing, graphic sex, FF/MF scenes, switching of control, minor bondage, minor edging, exhibitionism, and feeding during sex.

A Vow for the Vamp ends with a happily ever after. It will be the first book in a series of interconnected standalones featuring supernatural beings.

Help is available

Suicide & Crisis Lifeline — Call or Text: 988

https://988lifeline.org/

https://afsp.org/

https://nami.org/Home

National Domestic Violence Hotline: 800-799-7233 or

Text START to 88788

https://www.thehotline.org/

Please consider donating to St. Jude:

https://www.stjude.org/

Dedication

You are the sun to someone's darkness

Playlist

Girl You Know It's True - Milli Vanilli
If You Want My Blood (You've Got It) - AC/DC
Turn Off The Lights - Teddy Pendergrass
To Know You Is To Love You - BB King
Sunday Kind Of Love - Etta James
I Just Want To Make Love To You - Etta James
(Sittin' On) The Dock Of The Bay - Otis Redding
Love Man - Otis Redding
These Arms Of Mine - Otis Redding
You're My Latest, My Greatest Inspiration - Teddy Pendergrass

Listen Here:

Chapter 1 - Millie

I am going to leave this bar and yeet myself into traffic.

Why did I move to New York City? Albeit there weren't millions of people here in the 1850s. There was no technology. No crowded sidewalks with noses stuck in phones. No tourists suddenly stopping in front of you to take photos, just to post them on social media for clout, causing you to have to do a little dance to avoid running into them.

I've had enough.

Sure, I could move to the suburbs where there are fewer crowds. Or even the countryside where animals outnumber humans.

But that would mean my life would go on, and I'd *still* be miserable.

If I could die, I'd walk out into the street and let the next passing bus barrel into me.

I mean, I can die, but not by bus, or terminal illness, or even a knife to the stomach. Death by breaking my neck? Nope.

I have very few options: a wooden stake, or bullet, to the heart. My head, or heart, being ripped from my body. Or I could face the sun and burst into flames. All are extremely painful ways to die but not as painful as continuing to live this godforsaken life.

I'm so fucking bored.

Nothing excites me anymore. Music, movies, television shows, art, books, sex. Yes, I enjoy those things, but it's all beginning to blur.

I've experienced life to its fullest. I've traveled the world, learned all the languages, forgot all the languages, took classes for everything one could imagine:

Cannabis 101. How to Survive the Zombie Apocalypse. The Art of the Selfie. How to Waste Time on the Internet. TikTok for Millennials. Pinot and Paint. Pole Dancing. Young People Slang for Old People. Improv 101. Musical Improv 101. The Art of Paper Mache.

Five hundred years of living and hating my existence. And it's all because of the man who turned me.

I was thirty years old with a husband and two kids with plans for a third. We had just settled into our new home in the countryside north of London a few weeks earlier. It was after dusk, and I'd forgotten to bring in the laundry off the drying rack. Our new home was located on an isolated part of land with the nearest neighbor miles apart. Aside from wild animals frequently approaching our home looking for food, I had no reason to fear the night. I had no reason to look over my shoulder or be on guard.

I didn't know a vampire was watching me. Hell, I didn't even know vampires existed until one was sucking on my neck.

Heinrich, the fucker, had been wandering from village to village, killing humans for his entertainment. He found me alone outside, approached me from behind, and covered my mouth with his hand so I couldn't scream. He sunk his teeth into my neck and drank from me until I was weak and not able to fight back.

Not that I would have been able to fight him off at full strength.

Heinrich was cruel. I begged him for death. Instead, he kept me alive so I could watch my family die. I pleaded with the monster of the night to spare them. I bargained with him, telling him I'd do anything he wanted.

I never expected him to turn me.

After a couple hundred years, Henry—a name I started calling him because he loathed it—got bored of using me, abusing me, and ordering me to kill alongside him. He'd spend weeks away, sometimes months, and I eventually worked up the nerve to leave him. It wasn't easy. He was my sire, and I was bound to him.

But I found a way.

I moved to America because I knew it'd be the last place he'd search for me. Thankfully, all I needed to escape was my determination and a trunk full of clothes and personal items. Money was never an issue. I didn't need to buy food or lodging since vampires have the ability to charm a human into compliance.

Compulsion is the one good thing that came out of meeting Henry. I've been compelling my way into free rooms, lofts, and two-story homes for most of my life.

I've started many new lives because when you're a vampire, people begin to question why you're not aging like everyone else. Which is why I chose to move to New York City. It was a fast-growing metropolis, and as the years went by, the easier it was to disappear.

Now? It's too damn crowded.

I stare down at my brand-new dress where a wasted woman spilled her vodka cranberry drink on my chest, causing the sweet liquid to trickle onto my lap. This is what I get for wanting to get high tonight. Alcohol and drugs don't do shit for me, but drinking the blood of someone who's intoxicated or stoned does.

"Oh my God. I'm so sorry," the gorgeous blonde giggles, slapping a palm over her mouth. She holds out her other hand. "Let's go clean you up."

Perfect. My next meal.

She takes my hand, it's smaller than mine. Her skin is soft and warm and if she notices how cold I am to the touch, she doesn't say a word.

She's half my size too.

Being fat was never an issue when I was turned. I was immortalized with a soft and jiggly stomach, thick and cottage cheese thighs, stretch mark-riddled arms, and an extra chin. This body of mine was never seen as negative, and people certainly never shamed me for my size and loving my plentiful curves.

Now? I'm basically invisible. For a vampire, that works quite well when most of the world doesn't know about our existence.

Like right now. No one suspects I'm following the blonde into the bathroom to consume her blood. I'm just one of the girls, joining a friend for a pee break because these modern women rarely make solo trips to the restroom, especially when the night involves copious amounts of booze.

The moment we enter the single toilet room, I lock the door. The woman is at the sink, gathering paper towels and wetting them under the water. She turns and walks to me, a smile spreading across her face. She's young. At least twenty-four if I were to guess.

"Can I?"

I nod and without breaking eye contact with me, she slides the paper towel over the dress, from my cleavage and my stomach down to my crotch where the majority of the drink spilled. She rubs over the area, slowly at first, before picking up speed and putting pressure on my cunt. Then she secures a hand on my shoulder and walks us until my back hits the wall.

This woman is shorter than me. I'm five six. She has to be close to five feet, but our height and weight difference doesn't stop her from taking control—something I rarely hand over.

But there's something sexy about a woman who knows what she wants.

The paper towel drops to the floor, and she reaches her hand underneath the bottom of my dress to find my black laced panties soaked. She pushes the fabric aside.

"I've been watching you all night," she purrs and slides two fingers inside me.

She curls the tips, causing me to moan. I briefly close my eyes and lean my head back against the wood.

"You have?" I ask, breathless.

"Yes, baby, and you've barely glanced my way." She pouts, but it's hard to pay attention to what she's talking about as she pumps her fingers in and out of me like a goddamn expert.

"Are you saying..." *moan.* "You spilled that drink..." *Fuck.* "On purpose?"

She presses her thumb to my clit and massages, and because it's been a while since I've indulged in casual sex, I explode into an orgasm. While my body shakes with the release, she grabs my hair and pulls my head back to press a kiss to my neck.

"Mhm. Guess it worked."

She licks the spot she kissed and removes her fingers from my cunt. That mischievous smirk I spotted after she spilled the drink on me returns as she licks off my pleasure.

"Tasty," she says.

As she's at the sink washing her hands, I walk up behind her. I wrap an arm around her waist, cup her chin, and tilt her head. We lock eyes in the mirror, and I expect to see fear staring back at me, but maybe she's too drunk to notice mine have turned black.

I can smell her arousal.

She closes her eyes. "Do it. I know who you are. *What* you are. Bite me."

This has happened to me before. Fang chasers. People who know of our existence and seek us out. They get off when we feed from them, craving the adrenaline of having their lives in our hands.

I'm not sure how she knew I was a vampire. Maybe she recognized me because I'm considered important in my world. Fang chasers know all the high-profile vamps.

Whatever the reason, I don't care.

"What's your name?"

"Ana," she responds, her chest heaving and her hard nipples poking through the fabric of her top.

"Beautiful name, Ana. I'm going to bite you now, okay?" My voice lulls her into a hypnotic compliance. "You won't remember this tomorrow. Tomorrow you'll wake up after a fun night out drinking with friends. You had too much and got sick in the bathroom."

She may know of our existence, but I can't have her remembering my face. I definitely can't get caught feeding in public. I didn't care to follow any rules tonight since I don't plan to be around tomorrow. It's why I ditched my security team, something I do often when I want to be alone. Still, I don't want a dramatic exit. If I let Ana remember tonight, she might go around bragging about her bathroom hookup with a plus-size vamp with the midnight hair and silver and black eyes.

The eyes always give me away.

Ana nods, biting her lip. Her pupils dilate until all that is left is a ring of blue.

She gasps when my mouth descends on her neck, my fangs sliding out and piercing her skin. When her blood pours into my mouth, I moan the same time she does.

Damn, this is hot.

Once her eyelids start drooping and her heartbeat slows, I know she's close to passing out, and it's time to stop feeding.

I pull away and prick the pad of my thumb, dabbing my blood on the fang holes, then brushing her long hair over her shoulder to hide the bite. It will heal faster with my blood, but it'll take a couple hours to disappear.

"You were such a good girl," I say, and she turns around. She leans in for a kiss, but I hold up my finger. "Go back to your friends, tell them you threw up in the bathroom and you're going home. Keep your hair over your neck. Okay?"

With a nod, she leaves the bathroom.

I check my reflection, making sure I didn't make a mess of that feeding, then grab my clutch and walk out.

The bar has become packed with people, standing shoulder to shoulder as it nears nine at night. Now that I've fed—and came, thanks to Ana—I have no reason to stay.

Just under nine hours until dawn and I have a few loose ends to clear up before facing the sun.

I squeeze myself through hot bodies. Everyone's drunk or entranced in conversation and no one notices me struggling to slip out. By the time I reach the door, I'm agitated as hell and aggressively sling the door open... only for it to slam into something hard.

Not something... *someone.*

"Ow!" a deep voice says.

When I emerge, I find a blond man cupping his nose.

"Oh, shit, sorry," I say and try to keep walking.

He moves to block my path.

A coppery rust scent hits me, and my fangs drop despite feeding just minutes ago.

Fuck.

He's bleeding.

And it smells divine.

"That's all you have to say? Shit, sorry?" he asks, his voice muffled behind his hands as he conceals his injury.

I narrow my eyes at him. My cold stone stare typically scares people away as if they recognize the predator standing before them.

Not this man.

He straightens his shoulders and drops his arms, revealing his face. It's stained with streaks of blood from his nostrils, down his chin, to his light blue, short-sleeved, V-neck shirt.

He's taller than me, perhaps six foot to my five foot six. And he's big. Broad shoulders, wide chest, strong arms, but his stomach is a little soft. Not technically plus-size like me, but not ripped either.

A dad bod.

He smiles, blood staining his teeth too. It takes everything in me to retract my fangs and keep them there.

I've never smelled blood so delicious.

"Where are you heading in such a hurry?" He holds out his hand, his palm covered in blood. "I'm Teddy. You are...?"

"Sorry about your nose," I say, pulling a napkin from my cleavage and handing it to him. I keep them there in case I spill during feedings, but he needs it more. Especially since I'm seconds away from jumping this man and ripping his throat out so I can have a taste of that mouth-watering blood of his.

He takes the napkin and shakes his head—that irritating smile still on his handsome face—when he realizes I've rejected his greeting. I don't touch humans unless I'm feeding from them. Especially in the summer. My cold skin on a hot and humid night always garners too many curious questions.

Ana was the exception because I knew I'd be compelling her to forget.

"You got a box of tissues in your tits?" he asks and laughs.

His amusement lights up his face, his green eyes shining.

I typically can't stand happiness. Probably because I haven't been happy in centuries. But this man's energy is endearing. It could also be Ana's blood kicking in. Fuck. She had more than booze tonight. Drugs, definitely. Molly maybe? Ecstasy?

Whatever it is, it's making me horny. I find myself... attracted to this golden retriever man.

I'm horrified.

"No, I'm not storing *tissues* in my tits. I'm storing napkins. Now, if you'll excuse me, I must go—"

I try to walk around this man and once again he steps in my way.

I zero in on his eyes.

"You will move and let me pass. Then you'll go into that bar," I nod over my shoulder, "and clean yourself up. Do you understand me, young man?"

His eyes widen slightly before he bursts into laughter.

"Young man? You can't be much older than me."

What the hell? My compulsion didn't work? Is Ana's blood hindering the ability? No. That's not it. I *know* I've compelled humans while intoxicated before.

"Tell me your name." His voice is rough, full of demand, and my pussy pulses in response.

What the fuck?

"You at least owe me that for beating me up with a door."

I ignore the way my confused body is reacting to this man and pinch the bridge of my nose. "I didn't beat you up! It was clearly an accident."

Why am I defending myself to this stranger? To this *human?*

He stands there, arms crossed and that infuriating smile refusing to falter. The streaks of blood on his face only add to his appeal.

He could at least wipe the blood off his palms with the napkin I gave him. I'm practically foaming at the mouth for a taste.

His eyes trail down my body, pausing at my breasts where my traitorous nipples poke through the fabric of my red dress.

"Tell me," he commands, his voice dropping an octave.

I barely stifle my whimper.

Ok, seriously. What the hell is wrong with me?

You know what? Fuck it. What's a little more fun tonight when it's the last one I'll ever have? This man is gorgeous, and he seems to be into me—I'm most definitely into him. I'd planned to hook up with someone tonight anyway and if Ana hadn't been a fang chaser, it would have been her.

Maybe this puppy can be my last fuck and feed.

"Fine. You can have my name. It's Millie."

"Hello, Millie. Nice to meet you."

Chapter 2 - Teddy

What am I doing?

Why am I flirting with this stranger after she nearly killed me with a door?

Millie.

The moment she appeared in front of me, not an ounce of remorse on her beautiful face, a zing of excitement shot throughout my body. One grumpy look from her and I was smitten.

There's something... different about her.

She radiates power.

The way her eyes pierce through my soul—they're the lightest shade of blue with dark specks throughout—cause my heart to thunder against my chest and my cock to push against the zipper of my jeans.

Her long black hair is styled in curls, cascading over her shoulders, and I want to wrap it around my wrist and tug her head back so I can devour her mouth.

Her pale skin begs to be reddened.

And that body. Her tight red dress clings to her large breasts, soft stomach, thick thighs, and long legs.

I don't care if this woman is a cold-blooded killer; I'd gladly let her take me home and murder me.

Not that it matters if I die tonight.

My friends, Alex and Landon, have abandoned me, entering the bar Millie just left. I texted them earlier today asking if they wanted to hang out. I was going to tell them some pretty shitty news I learned today, then chickened out and decided tonight would be about numbing myself with booze and finding someone to fuck.

I never expected to meet someone so fast. I have decent luck when I go out. I'm an extrovert. I'll talk to anyone who smiles at me. Though this woman has yet to show me a smile. She actually seems annoyed by me.

Why do I find her grumpiness so hot? She's literally my opposite.

Maybe that's why I'm acting so... desperate right now. I *need* to make her smile. I *need* her to order me around again like she tried to do just minutes ago. It was hot as hell, and while I like to be in control in the bedroom, Millie is the type of woman I'd fall to my knees for and beg her to destroy me.

Would she let me take her home? It can't be anything more than a one-night stand.

Maybe two nights. Or three.

I have a feeling one night with this woman would be the equivalent of an hour. I'd need more.

"Can I buy you a drink?" I ask, nodding toward the bar.

Her adorable button nose scrunches.

"I've already had enough to drink tonight."

"A late-night meal? I passed by a diner a block back."

The corner of her mouth twitches and my heart beats a little too fast with excitement.

I *almost* made her smile.

"I'm not going anywhere with you looking like a horror show. Why haven't you used my napkin to clean up?"

I glance down at my light blue shirt covered in streaks of crimson. Wow. She really did a number on me. My fingertips graze underneath my nose and over my lips, still damp with blood. At least it's stopped gushing.

I open my hands and stare at my blood-covered palms, then notice the napkin on the ground. I didn't realize I dropped it.

Her eyes follow my line of sight.

"Oops." I say with a shrug.

Maybe she'll give me another boob napkin.

I suppose I could go clean up inside the bar. I eye the door.

Every time it opens, I spot bodies packed in like sardines. It's too crowded. I can't go in there like this. I'd certainly scare a few people. I mean, sure, I'd be able to wash the blood off my face, but not the shirt.

But it's also New York City and no one will bat an eye, likely seeing worse on the subway during their commute.

Millie must notice my internal battle and sighs, loud enough to let me know she's *definitely* annoyed with me.

Even though she's the one who hit *me* with a door.

"My place isn't far."

It's all she says before turning away and walking down the sidewalk.

I guess I'm going to her place.

My cock jerks at the thought.

"So, Millie," I begin when I finally catch up to her. "Are you from New York? You walk fast like a New Yorker."

"I'm from a lot of places, but New York has been my home for one hundred and—" She pauses before clearing her throat. "It seems like I've been here for hundreds of years."

"You don't have an accent, not a New York accent anyway. Actually, the way you say certain words almost sound

British. Is that where you're from? I'm from Kansas, a small town south of Topeka. Do you know where Topeka is? It's the capital. Anyway, I moved here about five years ago after college. Now I work in finance. It pays decent. Kinda boring and I work too many hours. Don't have much of a social life because of that. I mean, not that I'm a loser. I'm not. I... I don't think I am."

I curse myself for being a nervous wreck and rambling. Millie doesn't respond to anything I've just said. She's focused on walking, still fast enough that I'm almost jogging to keep up.

"Has anyone ever called you Milli Vanilli?"

She stops suddenly, and I nearly run into her back. She turns to face me, her eyebrows pinched.

"You know Milli Vanilli? How old are you?"

My heart races in my chest. Another music fan by chance? Why does that intimidate me? Maybe because I never find anyone with my level of music snobbery. Or maybe because I never delve into deep conversations about musical tastes and other interests with my hookups.

I don't do relationships. Commitment doesn't appeal to me. The idea of spending time with just one person sounds so... boring. Plus, sex is fun, and I have no issues getting it, so why would I stop for just one person?

Jesus. I'm so fucking full of myself. I'm not God's gift to women. I mean, sure, I'm handsome. At least, people have told me I am. I don't really care about looks. I find beauty in most everything.

A bag of trash: stinky, disgusting... but it contains life inside. The discarded containers that once contained the food that filled someone's stomach. The used tissues that maybe they used to wipe their tears after watching a sad movie... or to clean up after giving themselves pleasure.

Okay. I tend to keep these thoughts to myself because I know I sound like a tool.

But seriously, beauty is so subjective and for our society to dwell on appearances... it pisses me off.

"I'm twenty-nine. What about you?" I stifle a groan. Is it still rude to ask women their age? If she's offended, she doesn't let on.

"I'm thirty."

"Really? You seem younger. I'd have guessed twenty-six."

She snorts.

"Did I... did I just make you laugh?"

"It was a snort, not a laugh. I don't laugh. I just find it ridiculous that you think I'm younger."

She purses her plump lips, painted velvet red to match her dress. She may not have smiled or laughed, but I see amusement in her eyes. I'm obsessed with them. I've never seen a shade of blue so light, it appears more silver. They resemble the moon.

Standing underneath a streetlight, her pale skin seems to glow. It's... ethereal. Is she human? An angel?

I don't know how long I've been staring, and I hope she hasn't noticed the tent in my pants before she turns to keep walking.

"To answer your question, yes, I do know Milli Vanilli. But now I must ask you... do you know Teddy Pendergrass?"

Teddy Pendergrass?

Ok, her knowing Milli Vanilli lets me know she's into music, but she's into soul music too? An R&B fan?

"Someone knows their music."

"I'm old. Um, I mean an old soul. Thirty isn't old, obviously. I'm just saying, I love music from all generations, and I rarely meet anyone with my taste, so I'm surprised, is all."

We stop at a busy street corner, waiting for the little green man to appear, allowing us to cross. She stares straight ahead, fidgeting on her feet while she chews on her nails.

"Am I making you nervous?"

She scoffs. "I don't get nervous."

"You sure seem flustered."

"I am not."

"Turned on, maybe?"

She sighs.

"That wasn't a no," I say, raising a brow, but she avoids my questioning stare. "Well, you're cute when you squirm."

I'd love to make her squirm in other ways.

"Cute? I don't think I've ever been called cute before."

"I don't believe you."

"Cute, no. Sexy? Sure. Scary, most definitely."

I laugh because there's nothing I find scary about this woman. She's... stunning. Intimidating would be the better word to describe her.

There's something dangerous about her, but maybe that's because her weapon of choice is a door.

"Well, I love being scared."

I cringe the moment I say it. It's not true. I hate the dark and horror movies. I once went to a haunted house and ran out screaming the first time an actor, disguised as a zombie, popped up out of nowhere and began chasing me.

"Yeah? You like scary movies and haunted houses?"

"Absolutely."

"What about adventure?" she asks as we cross the street.

Ok. This one I can answer truthfully. I love the outdoors. Lakes, camping, whitewater rafting, hiking, and exploring in general.

"Adventure is my middle name. Theodore Adventure Thibodeaux."

She stops again and holds up a hand. "Wait. WAIT. Your name is Theodore?"

Why did I tell her my full name? I never introduce myself as Theodore. I actually can't stand the name.

"Yes?" I run my hand through my shaggy blond hair. Millie's eyes follow the movement, and I swear there's desire behind her stare. "It's old-fashioned. I was named after my great-grandfather. Is that a deal breaker?"

And then it happens. She smiles. It's brief but Lord it was beautiful.

"No. Not at all. My name is old-fashioned too. Mildred."

She rolls her eyes noticing *my* smile and turns to keep walking.

"Mildred. I like it." I say, jogging to catch up since she's a superhuman who walks like her ass is on fire.

"No one likes the name Mildred. It's why I go by Millie."

"That's a solid name too. You don't meet a lot of Millies nowadays. Or Mildreds. You're my first. You've popped my Millie-Mildred cherry."

She looks away, and I'm convinced it's to hide a smile from me.

"You know what?" she says, daring a glance at me. "I don't think I've ever met a Theodore, either."

"I'm honored to be your first."

We continue down a street in midtown where luxury high-rises reside. We've walked at least ten blocks at this point.

"I thought you said your place was close."

"It is. Just one more block."

I've realized since moving to the Big Apple that when New Yorkers say something is close or within 'walking distance,' they either mean a couple of blocks or fifteen.

We finally arrive at a modern building that's got to be at least forty stories tall. Maybe fifty. Hell, I don't know, but it's fucking tall.

"You... you live here?" I ask, speechless. "What do you do for a living?"

"It's old money."

A man in a tailored, long-sleeved jacket, matching black pants, and a midway cap waits, holding the door open for us. He nods as we pass. Another doorman with stark white hair and a few wrinkles stands behind a long, sleek desk just inside the lobby—which has to be double the size of my entire apartment.

"Miss Maycot," he says with a nervous smile.

I don't know if he's nervous because she's a goddess or because I look like I've just murdered someone.

I'm going to say it's her, because I'm nervous too. I'm never this anxious. About anything. I'm outgoing and make friends with everyone. I have no issues talking to people. So, why does Millie make me feel as if my nerves are about to explode?

Two big guys, decked out in suits, wait by the elevators. They nod to us, barely making eye contact.

"There are a lot of important people in this building," Millie says, obviously noticing me staring at them, confused.

Okay, so security is tight. Does that mean Millie is important too? The moment I laid eyes on her, I knew she was special, so I have no doubt she's someone with power.

Inside the elevator, she inserts a key card and pushes the button to the penthouse.

The penthouse?

Okay, so maybe Millie's a trust fund baby. I can't even imagine how much an apartment in this building would cost.

Millie Maycot. Mildred Maycot.

Who are you? I'm dying to find out more about this woman who has enthralled me since pummeling me with a door.

The elevator takes less than a minute and it opens to a foyer with white, gray, and black swirled marble floors. Artwork lines the walls—no doubt expensive—and a chaise lounge sits in a corner.

Two more men in suits stand at double wooden doors.

More security guards?

She's definitely important. A politician maybe? I hate watching the news. It's depressing as hell. I wouldn't know a politician if they were sitting next to me. She could be a celebrity. I rarely watch TV in general. Movies, sometimes, but not enough to recognize a star.

Maybe she's a princess. Or a queen.

No, wait. She said she's lived in New York for a while. She couldn't be royalty.

I cautiously follow her through the entrance. The place is dark, with a few lamps illuminating the hallway to my right and what appears to be the kitchen further in on the left.

"Are you bringing me here to murder me?"

"Don't be silly, Theodore."

Millie appears in front of me so suddenly, I stumble back.

She reaches out her hand, latching on to my forearm to keep me from falling. Her skin is cold, yet her touch ignites a fire inside my body, spreading wildly through my veins.

She pulls back her arm as if she felt it too.

"I didn't mean to scare you."

I shrug. "I told you; I like being scared."

She smirks and looks me up and down. I do the same. God. I've never seen such a beautiful woman before. I'm fighting back the urge to touch her again, my hands shaking with how desperately I want to hold her, kiss her, devour her.

She doesn't move as I step toward her. Can she see the hunger on my face?

"Can you feel that?" I ask, inches now separating us. She doesn't ask me to clarify, and to be honest, I'm not sure what I mean either, but she nods. "Can I kiss you?"

Millie stands taller. She's shorter than me, though she's wearing heels, adding to her height. I stare into her eyes. They're *unreal*. The blue essentially fades under the light, appearing more silver and vibrant up close.

"I want to kiss you," I repeat, the words nearly a whisper. But she heard them perfectly.

"Then kiss me."

"The blood..."

"I don't care."

She fists my shirt and brings me flush against her body.

She's the one who kisses *me*.

Chapter 3 - Millie

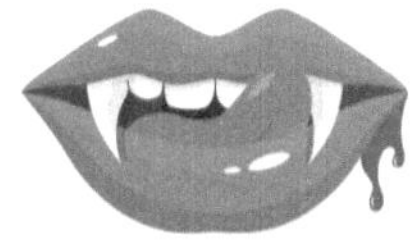

My lips collide with Teddy's.

They're soft, gentle, consuming.

It's not often my lovers treat me so delicately. I'm a big woman and most people feel that gives them the right to be rough. Don't get me wrong, I love it rough. But sometimes I want to be held like I'm about to break. As if I'm not a cold-blooded killer who's drained the life out of hundreds of people.

I don't need to kill to survive. I did it because I was forced to. I was compelled by my sire who convinced me it was fun... exhilarating... addictive. I let the power overtake me until I no longer needed to be compelled. Feeling someone's life fade, hearing their last heartbeat as I drained their blood, made me feel like a god. It's what I believed. It's what I was *tricked* to believe.

I was no god. I was a monster.

It's what Henry made me to be.

Controlling myself around humans hasn't been an issue for centuries. Yet that feral need to devour Teddy ignites within my body and climbs up my throat. He presses his hard cock against my soft stomach, and I moan into his greedy mouth.

His blood is *intoxicating*.

It's only a taste, whatever stained his lips from his nosebleed, but it leaves me panting for more. I've drunk the blood of many humans over my lifetime, and no one has ever made my body feel so... *heated*.

I need to stop before I kill him.

I press my palm on his chest and gently push. He pulls away, breathing heavily, and the blush on his face deepens.

I cover my mouth with my hand, hiding my fangs—which refuse to stay sheathed—and his blood now smeared on my lips and chin.

"I'm sorry. Was that... Did I..."

"You did nothing wrong. I just... need to slow down or I might just eat you up," I say jokingly.

I'm *not* joking.

Teddy smiles, combing his fingers through his blond locks. "You're right. I was seconds from tossing you onto the couch and—"

I hold my finger over his lips because if I let him finish that sentence, I'll take my chances and let him have his way with me.

"Let's get you cleaned up," I say, turning away before he can focus on my black eyes. They darken when I'm aroused, and I don't want to scare him away just yet.

I lead him down a long hallway to a guest bathroom and grab a towel from the storage closet.

"I'll find you a change of clothes," I say and set the towel on the counter.

I step out, waving my hand at the bathroom, and he goes inside, closing the door but leaving it open a crack.

I head to a spare bedroom where I keep a closet full of clothes—most are mine that I love, but no longer wear. But I also keep a few outfits on my shelves for situations like this where I bring a human into my home and, for whatever reason, they need a change of clothes.

Though, I've never been in *this* specific situation where I hit a man with a door and cause his nose to bleed all down the front of his body.

I find a pair of jeans that I hope are his size and a T-shirt. It's a Milli Vanilli concert shirt from 1990, a year after the infamous lip-syncing incident revealed they weren't actually singing their own songs.

It was a bummer, but the songs are still fire.

I'll say I found the shirt at a thrift store in Brooklyn, but I actually bought it at their live show in Philly. I wore it once or twice, then stored it away.

I knock on the door and Teddy immediately opens it. Shirtless.

My eyes take in his body. He's a beefy man with stocky arms, tree trunk thighs, and a stomach that's not defined by abs.

"Millie," he whispers, witnessing me checking him out.

I hold out the clothes to him.

"I wasn't sure if you needed jeans so…"

He takes the pile. "Thank you. Do you want—"

"Something to drink?" I ask, interrupting whatever he was about to say. If it was to ask me to join him in the bathroom, I would have jumped on the opportunity.

Why am I acting like this? I'm all but drooling over this man. Certainly, Ana's blood wasn't *that* potent.

"Um, sure. I'll have whatever you're having."

"I don't think you'd like—never mind. I'll grab you a beer."

"Beer is good. I'll be out in a second," Teddy says.

I leave before I can ravish the man in the bathroom and head to the kitchen.

I don't need a kitchen. The cabinets are bare of food and cookware. I have a fridge, but it's full of artificial blood manufactured by scientists employed by WOVE, the World Organization of Vampire Elites. It's not sustainable, but it helps satiate the cravings in case of emergencies where I can't find a blood donor in time. I'm also old enough that I don't need to feed as often.

Vampires outnumber blood donors. Only a few hundred humans have signed up to willingly let us feed from them. That's compared to around 2,000 vampires living across all five boroughs of New York City—at least the ones who've registered with WOVE, which is required, but not every vamp follows the rules.

While vampires can't eat human food, we do consume alcoholic beverages: hard liquors, wine, beer. It may not get us wasted, but many of us enjoy the taste and it doesn't make us sick like food. For some vamps, like me, it reminds me of my humanity. Of a time before I was undead, and I'd enjoy a glass of red at dinner or some whiskey that my husband picked up during a trip to London.

It's been a few months since I've entertained a human, but I still have some beer stocked in my fridge and bottles of liquor on my bar cart. I grab Teddy a craft beer—he seems like the type to enjoy a local brew—and I twist the top off, then pour myself a glass of wine.

"I can't believe you have this Milli Vanilli shirt," Teddy says, returning to the living room.

I hand him his drink. "A thrift shop score."

The shirt barely fits him. The fabric clings to his chest and stomach, and I avert my eyes because Ana's blood has me wanting to jump his bones with every glance.

I didn't look away fast enough because he definitely caught me checking him out again. He smiles, ear to ear, which makes my stomach twist with... butterflies?

Well, that hasn't happened in... ever? Not that I can remember, at least.

Teddy takes a swig of his drink and strolls into the living room to begin exploring my penthouse. He walks around slowly, taking in the eclectic decor. The paintings I've collected over the years are originals, some handed over to me by the artists themselves like Rembrandt, Delacroix, and Manet. I also have pieces from Van Gogh and Monet, acquired after their deaths since I had already moved to New York City when their work became successful and neither artist traveled to the U.S.

The one Picasso piece I own I bought in the fifties from an anonymous seller. I always suspected it was Pablo himself. He was banned from visiting the U.S. for being part of the French communist party, but rumors swirled for years that he secretly visited the U.S. many times, including New York City.

"Holy shit. Are these real?"

"They are."

Teddy's eyes greedily take in the paintings, admiring their beauty for several minutes, not letting a single brush stroke go unseen.

He moves on to the sculptures adorning my bookcases, inspecting each one as if they hold all the secrets of the world. My book collection entrances him next. He traces a finger over the spines, reading every single title.

"Are these first editions?"

"Some, yes."

"Wow," he whispers. "You really are rich."

I don't correct him. I *have* accumulated a fortune in my five hundred years of living; however, many of those first edition books were bought for pennies when the authors were just starting out.

"No way," he gasps when coming upon my vinyl record collection. "I knew you were a music fan."

He sets his beer down on a table behind him and sifts through the stacks, every so often pulling a rare album out to marvel over.

"Of course you have this one." He holds up a *Girl You Know It's True* LP by Milli Vanilli. I smile, but roll my eyes, surprised that I'm finding a human amusing.

Thankfully, he didn't see my smile. I can't have him thinking I enjoy his company.

Why not?

I shake the thought and join him at the bookcase.

Teddy whistles and holds another record up. "This AC/DC LP has to be worth $10,000."

"Mmm, more like $5,000," I say, stopping short of telling him I bought it on release day for a couple dollars.

"*If You Want Blood (You've Got It)* is such a badass song."

"It might be my anthem."

Teddy laughs. Again, I'm not joking.

"Oh!"

This man's energetic energy is so... *potent*. I've never felt such an explosion of life in another person. He's like a hyper puppy.

My little golden retriever.

He pulls out my copy of *The Best of Teddy Pendergrass* and walks over to the player.

"Can I?"

"Be my guest."

He sets it up, placing the needle in the spot to play *Turn Off the Lights.*

He holds out his hand.

"Dance with me."

The words are more of an order than a request and my body obeys.

I place my hand in his, and he flinches, which I know is from my cold touch, but he doesn't question me about it and swings me around in a twirl. His arm snakes around my back and he tugs me against his body. Teddy Pendergrass starts singing and *my* Teddy belts out the words along with him.

My Teddy.

I don't even know why that thought crossed my mind.

We slow dance to the smooth notes of the song, and I melt at the fact that he's treating me so sweetly and delicately again.

Teddy's lips ghost across the skin of my neck, his breath warm. It smells like cinnamon toothpaste, and it mixes with the heady scent of his cologne. Nothing expensive, but there's a woody, somewhat fruity undertone. Grapefruit, maybe, and the forest after a fresh rain.

My cheeks would be blushing if I had a heartbeat to move blood throughout my body.

"You smell amazing," Teddy whispers and places a gentle kiss on my neck. He inhales deeply. "Like peaches and something floral."

Love Spell by Victoria's Secret. It's one of my favorite perfumes. Designer fragrances never appealed to me.

Teddy's palm smooths up and down my back before sliding lower to my ass.

"Tell me to stop and I will," he nearly growls. When I don't say a word, he continues, grabbing a handful and squeezing.

I moan.

"Why do I feel so drawn to you?" Teddy asks, and I pop my eyes open.

Yeah, why are we so addicted to each other after just meeting? I have drunk and drugged blood running through my veins. What's Teddy's excuse?

The song ends, and I step back out of Teddy's embrace.

"What is it? What's wrong?" Teddy asks, trying to reach for me. I dodge his hand and further the distance between us. He frowns.

"I think we need to set some boundaries."

He opens his mouth, then closes it.

"I just mean that I'm not looking for a commitment."

He rakes his hand through his hair, something I've noticed he does a lot. "Yes, right, of course. I can't do commitment either."

A strange way of saying that, but I'm glad we're on the same page.

"Then tonight will be about fucking," I continue.

"Yes. Just sex."

"Good."

He stands there, hands on his hips, staring at me as if waiting for me to make a move. But for some reason, my body wants to be dominated by this man. I want *him* to make the move. When he realizes this, his entire demeanor changes. His bright and sunny smile is still there, but his eyes have darkened.

"Tell me, Millie. What would you like me to do to you?"

He walks toward me, a fire igniting in his green eyes.

"You seem like the type of woman who likes to take control."

"I am."

"Hmm."

Once he's standing in front of me, he grabs my hair at the nape and tugs back hard enough to make me whimper.

"But you're letting me take control now. Why?"

"I'm curious."

He's a burnt cinnamon roll. I just know it. Ooey and gooey and full of sweetness but with charred edges. This sunshine man likes a little darkness. Maybe it's how he demanded my name outside the bar. How he insisted I dance with him just now, not even asking. And now as he wraps his long, thick fingers around my throat, squeezing not-so-gently.

My nipples pebble and cunt pulses because I've somehow become the prey.

"Was I right? About giving you control?"

"Yes. I need it, especially in the bedroom." He licks my neck. "Will you submit to me tonight?"

He sucks on the same part of my skin he just licked, and my fangs drop down against my will. This man is making it impossible to keep them sheathed, something I've been struggling with all night.

"Will you get on your knees for me? Comply with my orders?" His free hand skates down my body to the hem of my dress, which only reaches mid-thigh. "Will you let me fuck you until you're begging to come?" His finger-tips push aside my panties and tease my entrance. "Is that something you want, Millie? Tell me yes and I'll continue."

"Yes," I say, breathless.

He thrusts a finger into me, causing me to scream out a moan.

Fuck! When did I become submissive? That's twice now tonight. First with Ana, now Teddy. I'm the one with the paddles and handcuffs in my closet. I love tying my lovers to the bed so I can do as I please with them.

But this man went from day to night in a matter of minutes, and I'm *eager* to see just how dark he can go.

He fucks me with his fingers, bringing me to the cusp of orgasm before stopping and removing them. My fangs slide out *again*. This time it's because he's edging me, which equally pisses me off and turns me on.

He walks away before noticing and sits on my couch, arms spread over the back like a fucking boss.

"Undress and crawl to me," he orders.

I kick off my heels first, then unzip my dress. Slowly, I peel the fabric off my body.

"So," I begin, a smirk tugging at my lips. "This side of you..."

"Did I say you could talk?"

This fucking *brat*.

Once the dress is in a puddle on the ground, I remove my bra and panties. Teddy sucks in a sharp breath only he'd be able to hear if it wasn't for my enhanced hearing—one of the side effects of vampirism.

"Tell me," I say and drop to my hands and knees.

He purses his lips, considering not saying anything, but I refuse to move unless he speaks. He narrows his eyes, letting me know I'll be punished for my disobedience.

I look forward to it.

"I grew up in a loving home, but my parents were very strict. They didn't allow me to watch TV or play video games. All I had was music."

Okay, that makes sense why he loves music so much.

I begin crawling towards him slowly, so I can hear the rest of the story.

"They controlled everything I did, down to the friends I was allowed to have. I couldn't date. I didn't even lose my virginity until college."

He watches my every move, his breathing becoming labored and his heartbeat erratic.

Music to my ears.

"Fucking one person wasn't enough. I needed more, almost like I had to prove myself... to prove I was normal after the way I was raised. I became addicted to sex. I mean, not to a point that I needed help, but I fucked a lot. Women. Men. I love giving pleasure to my partners, but in my own way. A way that I can control."

He sounds like me. I spent too many years being controlled by Henry. Then, when I became free of him, I wanted to live my life on my terms, and that included exploring my sexuality.

I reach Teddy on the couch, placing my hands on his meaty thighs. I rub them up and down.

"Then tell me what to do, Theodore."

Chapter 4 - Teddy

Theodore.

That's the second time she's called me that.

Growing up, I hated it. My parents punished me with that name. Once I moved away to college and gained my freedom, I became Teddy.

Yet hearing Millie call me Theodore doesn't upset me or trigger all those painful childhood memories.

It's almost like she's redefining that part of my life. Making it hers.

Making it ours.

Millie reaches for my jeans and locks eyes with me. She slowly slides the zipper open, and I lift my hips to help her tug down the material, along with my boxer briefs. My hard dick springs free.

"Do you want me to suck your cock? Let you come down my throat?"

I groan and stop her hands from wrapping around my shaft.

"While I love seeing you on your knees before me... I'd much rather your first orgasm be from riding me. I want to see your face when you fall apart."

This woman will be my undoing. I rarely meet someone who's as comfortable in their own skin and sexuality as I am. She knows what she wants.

She knows exactly what she's doing.

"May I mount you then, *sir*?"

I narrow my eyes at the way she says sir.

She's mocking me.

She's being a brat, egging me on so I'll punish her.

I curl my finger, ordering her to get on my lap.

She straddles me, immediately stripping me of my shirt. I hiss the moment she places her freezing hands on my shoulders. Our kiss, the dance, my hand around her throat—every time my skin meets hers, I shiver. I open my mouth to question her about her cold touch, but she covers my mouth with hers. Words melt away as she laps her tongue over mine.

Without breaking the kiss, she smooths her palms down my chest and over my stomach before reaching for my cock.

My entire body is on fire, and I groan at the welcome chill from her hands as she wraps her fingers around me. She's seconds from sinking down my length when I stop her.

"Shit." I glance over my shoulder. "I have a condom in my pants, which I left in the bathroom."

"I don't want one—"

"Oh, thank God," I say and thrust up into her.

Millie screams when I fill her to the hilt. The pleasure is consuming. Exaggerated in a way I can't explain. I almost come when her pussy throbs around me.

She clutches my shoulders for leverage and lifts until only the tip of my cock is inside her, then she sinks back down.

"Fuck, Millie, this feels... fuck!"

She repeats the motion again and again, sliding up and down my dick, then rotating her hips in circles.

I lean in and cover her nipple with my mouth, sucking it in and flicking my tongue over the sensitive bud.

She cries out, her cunt gripping my cock at the move. I don't let up, sucking harder and scraping my teeth over one nipple while I tweak the other between my fingers.

She buries her hands into my hair, latching on and tugging painfully on the strands.

While my mouth worships her breasts, I skim both my palms around to her backside and take handfuls of her plentiful ass.

Then I hold her in place and take over, driving into her at a punishing pace. Every sound that comes out of her mouth—moans, groans, whimpers—fuels me on.

I crash a hand down on her ass and she cries out. I swallow the sound with my mouth. My tongue clashes with hers and when I deepen the kiss, she bites down on my lip.

I groan, tasting blood, but I don't pull away. She sucks on my lips, greedily swiping her tongue as if she's licking up every last drop.

It's erotic as fuck, and I pound into her harder.

"Yes, Teddy," she mumbles against my mouth.

She's getting close. Her pussy walls constrict around me. When she's seconds from exploding with release, I stop moving and fill her to the hilt.

"What the fuck?" she growls, making me chuckle.

"I'm sorry. Did you want to come?"

"Yes!"

"Maybe you shouldn't have been asking me questions when I didn't give you permission to speak."

She rolls her eyes, and I spank her again. Her head falls back with a moan.

"Let me come!"

She tries to move her hips, but I tighten my hold on her.

"Don't. Move." Her cunt pulsates at the command.

I reach between us and find her swollen clit. She gasps when I press down, massaging it in circles. Her eyelids flutter and she squirms, disobeying my order to stay still. I set her up for failure with that move. I'm also confident Millie doesn't like to be told what to do.

I take her nipple into my mouth again and bite down, just hard enough to cause pain.

"Oh God, Teddy!"

I realize I should have asked her for a safe word in case this got to be too much. Everyone's limits are different. However, something tells me Millie is stubborn and would have refused a safe word.

"Good and patient girls are rewarded," I say with a smirk. She clenches her teeth, letting me know she does *not* want to be a good girl.

I adjust us to lay her back on the couch, still inside her, refusing to move. Her hands fall to my ass, and she squeezes, a silent command to start fucking her.

I pull out, slowly, then slide back into her just as gently.

She growls in frustration, and I respond by withdrawing and slamming into her... and staying put.

"You always get what you want, don't you, Milli Vanilli?"

"Yes," she whines.

Withdraw. Slam. Stay put.

"Do you ever beg for what you deserve?"

She shakes her head.

Withdraw. Slam. Stay put.

I slap her aching nipple with my next thrust and she cries out.

"Please," she wheezes.

I tsk. "One little word? That's all I get?"

Withdraw. Slam. Stay put.

"Teddy, please, sir. Fuck me harder. Faster. Let me come. I need you to give me my release."

I chuckle.

"You're so bad at begging." I pull out nearly all the way. "But you're trying so I'll give you what you ask."

I piston my hips, shaking her body with every brutal thrust. She's getting close again, since I've been edging her. When I pin her hands over her head, she arches her back off the couch.

She liked that. I should tie her up next time.

Next time? I'm getting ahead of myself.

We only agreed to one night. No commitment.

Just sex.

My balls tighten, preparing to come, and Millie's cunt does the same and with a few more pumps, she's shaking with an orgasm.

I still, reaching my release, and let my cum pour inside her.

I'm panting and sweating, and I lean my forehead on her chest between her breasts.

"You're cold. Always so cold. How is that possible?" I ask, out of breath. "I'm sweating and hot as hell."

She hums. "You did all the work."

"Still..."

"I'm cold blooded."

I lift my head, frowning and open my mouth to question that, but she pushes at my chest.

"I need to clean up."

"Let me."

She pauses at the words. "What?"

"Let me take care of you." She carefully lifts herself off me and I stand, holding out my hand.

"I don't understand," she says, her face twisting with doubt.

"Has no one ever cleaned you up after sex?"

Her eyes widen. "I suppose not."

She takes my offered hand and I lead her to the bathroom. I grab a washcloth and run it under warm water before kneeling in front of her.

My cum is dripping out of her and I'm tempted to push it back inside. I don't know why that thought crosses my mind. I always wear protection. The way I grew up, getting married and having children... a family... didn't seem fathomable. I was terrified I'd become like my parents.

Millie makes me feel... territorial. I want to claim her as mine. My cum belongs to her now. I want it inside her. *All* of it.

I shake my head because I *can't* have her.

Her fingers comb through my hair. "What are you thinking about? Or are you just that focused on cleaning your cum from my cunt?"

I smile and clear my throat.

"I was just thinking about how you're the first person I've fucked without a condom and..."

"Ah. Do you regret it?"

I finish my aftercare and kiss her thick thighs before standing. I cup her face in my hands and cover her mouth with mine.

This kiss is soft, slow, worshipping. Unlike the frantic and hungry kisses we shared during what has to be the best sex I've ever had.

"No. It was amazing... almost intoxicating if that makes sense," I say when we part.

She palms my cheek and I shiver, *again*. It's unnatural how cold her skin is, but I've already tried asking her about it. She's avoiding answering.

"Come on. Let's get dressed, and find you some food. If we're having a one-night stand, then it's not over until the sun rises. It's barely ten, so we have several hours left. I'm going to need you fueled."

She takes my arm and leads me out of the bathroom.

"Are you saying you want to fuck until the sun comes up?"

"That's exactly what I'm saying."

Chapter 5 - Millie

This is a bad idea. I'm already liking this hyperactive puppy way too much to let him go at the end of the night.

He *almost* makes me want to stay, but I can't. He would grow old and die as I stayed the same age.

You could turn him.

I startle at the thought. I swore to never turn a human after I was forced to live this life without my consent. Even the humans who beg me, I refuse. They have no idea what they're asking for. Becoming a vampire means never going outdoors to see the sunrise again. Never feeling your heart race when you're excited or scared. People you love will die. They'll be at peace while you go on to live forever and never age.

It's unnatural. Life becomes repetitive. Life becomes boring.

My one and only friend, Layla, hates that I feel this way. For her, being turned saved her life. She was living in Spain, on her deathbed with the bubonic plague, when her husband paid a vampire to save her.

Vampires don't like to drink the blood of humans sick with infections. It makes us ill as well. It won't kill us, but we become weak for days. But Layla said the moment the vampire saw her, he became obsessed.

Vampires don't fall in love. We fall into possession. We find a human we want and claim them. Before there were rules, many humans didn't survive a vampire encounter. Now, if they're lucky, they'll be compelled and let go and forget all about the supernatural world. Or the vampire will become so infatuated that they'll turn the human who then becomes immortal and develops a lust for blood.

It's sick, and I won't do it.

But Layla was dying, so she didn't protest. Her husband offered the vampire extra money to turn him, too, but Layla needed a human to feed on to complete the turn. She attacked her husband, killing him—revenge for years of abuse. Then, a few weeks later, she plunged a wooden stake into her sire's chest. A difficult and painful thing for a fledgling still bound to their sire to do.

But Layla wasn't going to let another man control her.

She was given a second chance, and she embraced this life as most vampires do. However, I cannot fathom playing God and choosing who gets to live forever.

I was given forever, and I barely lasted five hundred years.

Would the next five hundred be different if I had Teddy by my side?

I shake my head, quickly changing into a pair of sweats and a shirt while Teddy dresses in the living room. How can I have that thought about a stranger, a human, when it's barely been two hours since we met? I can't explain it. I'm attracted to him, sure, and I could blame my exaggerated horniness on Ana's booze and drug-infused blood, but I know it's more than that.

Nothing in my world is ever that simple.

However, there's no use investing in this connection if it will be severed at sunrise.

Returning to the kitchen, I open my fridge and frown. Right. I don't have food here.

"It appears I need to go grocery shopping," I say when Teddy joins me after getting dressed. "We could order in. Pizza?"

"Sounds good to me. I like everything. Except anchovies."

Teddy laughs, his entire face lighting up with sunshine. A tinge of jealousy rips through my chest.

I wish I could enjoy life as he does. Teddy's joy is natural. I've noticed any small moment garners a smile.

How I yearn to view the world through his eyes. Does he cherish every second as if it's his last? He'd mentioned how controlling his parents were growing up. He spent years experiencing life in a limited capacity.

Is his dark past what brightens his present?

"Do you ever get angry?" I ask, grabbing my phone to pull up the website for the pizza place down the block to order a pepperoni pie.

"Sometimes." He shrugs. "I find being angry is a waste of time and energy. Not always, but in most situations. Shit happens, and it's often an issue out of our control. Why get mad or upset about it? How does that help? Especially when mistakes are made by someone who is likely overworked and underpaid. We are surrounded by strangers dealing with their own personal emergencies and adding fuel to the fire will only make it worse."

"You're a better person than me," I say, in awe of this empathetic and compassionate man.

He leans his hip on the kitchen island and crosses his arms.

"Or maybe I don't get angry because I just like to smile. Maybe I want people to find me irresistible or charming or handsome because of that smile."

I raise a brow. "Is that why I brought you home? Your irresistible and charming smile?"

"Yes. And because you felt guilty for assaulting me with a door."

"I did not—" I clamp my mouth shut and turn back to the fridge to hide my smile. "The pizza will be here in thirty minutes. Would you like something to drink while we wait?"

"Sure! Surprise me."

He walks away, heading straight to my record player. He sifts through the stack sitting next to it—my favorite albums—and pauses halfway through.

Which one did he choose?

He removes the vinyl from the sleeve and carefully places it on the player. He treats it with such care. Just as he did with me after we fucked.

I'm not like a human who needs aftercare to prevent UTIs. I just didn't want to get cum on my couch. I was shocked when Teddy offered to clean me up. It's not something vampires do.

We fuck and feed and leave.

Wait.

Teddy and I fucked... but I didn't feed on him.

My fangs kept dropping, and I even bit him during our kiss, but I had no desire to feed from him.

I mean, I *do* want to drink his blood. It's delectable. But my body didn't crave it as much as it desired his *sex*.

If we plan to fuck until dawn, making the most out of our one-night stand, I won't be able to hide what I am from him much longer. My cold skin already has him suspicious. I could reveal myself then compel him to forget, but I'm hesitant after my compulsion failed earlier tonight—something I still cannot explain.

The familiar notes of BB King's *To Know You Is To Love You* fill the apartment.

Teddy returns to the kitchen and stops a foot from me. He starts solo dancing to the beat of the song, dipping his shoulders and shuffling his feet.

Crap that's adorable.

He really is irresistible and charming. I find him incredibly sexy, and I *rarely* have this unadulterated desire for another being, especially a human.

"Come on," he says. "Dance with me."

I'm in the middle of pouring us glasses of wine to pair with our pizza and shake my head.

"I don't dance."

"Yes, you do. We danced earlier."

"That was slow dancing. I don't do this..." I wave my finger in front of him.

He reaches out a hand and thankfully I'm saved by my phone ringing.

Wait. The pizza shouldn't be here already. I just placed the order.

"Are you going to answer that?" Teddy asks when I don't move. "It could be the pizza."

"It said thirty minutes, and it's only been five, and that's how long it takes just to walk to my apartment from the restaurant."

Besides, I know who's calling. I requested no interruptions tonight as it was going to be my last. Only one brave person would defy that request.

The ringing stops, and it's immediately followed by someone banging on the door.

"Sounds important."

I curse.

"Stay right here. *Don't* move."

"Yes, ma'am."

Yes ma'am?

I pause because the last time someone called me ma'am was decades ago when I was traveling through the South. Teddy did say he's from Kansas. Do people in the Midwest say ma'am there too?

He's too sweet. Too polite.

I'm going to corrupt him.

"What?" I seethe when opening the penthouse door a crack. "I told you not to interrupt me tonight, no matter what."

"I'm sorry, Your Majesty," my royal advisor says, trying to peer into the apartment to see what I'm hiding. "But we've received word that a feral vampire is leaving bodies across the city."

"Shh!" I hiss and open the door just enough to squeeze out.

I nod to my security guards standing on either side of the door, then narrow my eyes at my best friend.

I met Layla Sofia Aldana about one hundred years ago. Our connection is rare. Vampires don't tend to have close friends, at least not in the way a human would. But Layla is the type of person who draws you in, not only with her beauty, but her wit and aura. She radiates happiness, and while I'm her complete opposite, she's the only brightness I allow in my life. If she were any brighter, she'd rival the sun.

She's older by a couple hundred years with light brown skin and umber hair that's always up in a high ponytail. She's curvy, but not nearly as thick as me. People often underestimate her. She may be short, but she's fierce. And she's a badass fighter.

She once took out an entire team of vampire hunters all by herself, just to protect me. It's why I named her my right-hand woman.

"Who are you hiding in there?" she asks, reaching for the door. I swat her hand.

"No one. Go away. Don't make me sic the griffins on you."

My guards roll their eyes because they know I would never do that. Plus, I'm pretty sure Layla intimidates them.

Layla ignores my threat and sniffs the air, then scrunches her nose. "You smell like sex…" Her brow quirks. "Oh and with a man?" She sniffs some more, and her brown eyes widen. "A *human* man?"

"I do fuck men, occasionally. Humans too."

Layla is like me. We enjoy the company of all genders. We met in New Orleans at a jazz club. She was on stage singing in her sparkling flapper dress.

She was *stunning*.

We soon became an item. Our relationship was fueled by attraction. It was the 1920s and casual sex was growing in popularity. It was some of the best years of my life because Layla had quickly become my dearest friend. We had many things in common, including suffering years of being controlled by men.

After a months' long affair, we decided friendship would be best. Neither of us wanted to lose this connection and sex often ruins that part of a relationship.

It was for the best. She's too optimistic about life, whereas I'm hours away from ending it all.

I haven't told her.

I won't.

I did, however, write a recommendation to COVE, the Council of Vampire Elites, that she be named queen in my place. They'll find it in my will, which also leaves my entire estate to Layla. Not that she needs it. She has her own wealth and belongings. But she's the only one I trust with my legacy.

"Who is it?"

"No one. Again, mind your business."

"I am your business, Millie May."

I groan. "You know I hate when you call me that."

"Fine, *Your Majesty*. So what do you want to do about the feral vampire? Should I call the gargoyles?"

I shift on my feet and nibble on my bottom lip.

"Yes. Have them be on the lookout." I sigh. "I suppose I should send my one-night stand home so you can tell me everything you have on this vampire. It's been a couple years since we've had one go mad with blood lust."

I open the door and walk back inside, only to come face to face with Teddy. I freeze in place, and Layla bumps into me.

"What the hell?" she grumbles.

"Um…" Teddy says, standing in the foyer near the penthouse entrance where he *definitely* heard what we were talking about. "Vampires? Blood lust?"

"Shit," I say.

"Shit," Layla echoes.

Chapter 6 - Teddy

"**A**re you... a vampire?" I ask the woman I just fucked... who's deathly pale and cold to the touch.

It's all making sense.

A part of me knew something was different about Millie. The way she speaks sometimes... as if she's experienced hundreds of years of living despite appearing to be a thirty-year-old woman.

Her penthouse. Old money. Of course! The art on her walls, the memorabilia on her shelves. Her love for music.

She was there. She lived through these eras. She didn't buy antiques; she bought those items brand new.

"That's absurd," Millie says and approaches me.

I swallow the lump in my throat. Sweat lines my forehead and soaks my shirt. *Her* shirt. I've subconsciously been backing away, and now I'm in the kitchen. My back hits the island. Either Millie really is a vampire or she's part of some vampire worshipping cult that wants to sacrifice me to their God.

Either way, I'm going to die tonight.

I curse. My cock hasn't gotten the message that we're scared because it jerks at her nearness and her wonderfully sweet floral smell.

Wait. I fucked a vampire?

Why do I find that hot?

She locks eyes with me, and my heart responds by drumming inside my chest. She smirks.

Can she hear it beating?

Of course she can; she's a vampire.

"You're going to forget about tonight," Millie begins. My head throbs at her words, my vision blurring. Her voice becomes muffled, like she's talking under water, but I can still understand what she's saying. It's the same sensation outside the bar earlier tonight when she tried to order me inside. "Go home and go to sleep. Tomorrow you'll wake up and remember taking a woman home, but you were too drunk to recall her name or where she lives."

When she stops speaking, I blink, and everything clears.

"Um... what?"

She jerks back as if I've slapped her.

"It didn't work," she whispers.

"What didn't work? Millie." I sigh. "What is going on? I'm freaking the fuck out."

The woman who walked in with Millie steps in front of her. She does the same thing, locking her brown eyes with mine and repeating what Millie just said.

This time, I almost believe the words, but the moment she stops speaking, I shake my head.

"Are you two trying to hypnotize me or something?"

They share a glance before Millie takes my arm and pulls me to a stool, sitting me down. Okay, she's definitely a vampire. Her grip is strong, almost bruising, and if I tried to peel myself from her hold, I wouldn't be able to.

Where was this strength when we fucked?

I can't believe I had sex with a vampire.

I swallow to wet my dry throat. I'm trying not to panic at the fact that *vampires are real.* I take in deep breaths, but that only results in me inhaling more of Millie's scent.

Now is not the time to get a boner, Teddy!

"His heart is racing," the other woman says, amused.

Millie goes to the fridge and removes a beer, twisting the cap off as if it was nothing. She slides the bottle over to me.

I chug it halfway down.

"What are you?" Millie asks, watching me wipe away the beer that spilled on my chin. Her silver eyes light up at the movement and she licks her lips.

Silver eyes. I thought they were light blue when we met. Why wouldn't I think they were blue? No one has silver eyes. Wait. I'm pretty sure they were darker, black almost, when we were fucking. I assumed it was her pupils dilating because she was turned on. To be fair, I also wasn't thinking clearly while my cock was inside her perfect cunt.

Wait.

Does she have black eyes because she's an undead demon from hell?

"What am I?" I ask, my voice an octave higher. "What are you? You're the one talking about feral vampires and attempting to hypnotize me or some shit and..." I wave my hand up and down her body. "Looking like a sexy vampire queen with your silver eyes that I'm ninety percent sure turned black while we fucked and OH MY GOD."

My fingers ghost over my lips. It still stings when I press down.

"You bit me! And you sucked on my lip! You drank my blood!"

"He talks a lot, doesn't he?" asks the smiling woman standing next to Millie. "Like an overactive golden retriever puppy. So much energy."

"Yeah," Millie chuckles, arms crossed. "I find it rather charming, to be honest."

She lifts her hand, and I flinch, which makes her frown. She continues on until she's brushing back a piece of my hair that's fallen into my eyes.

"I'll ask again," she says, her fingernails scraping over my scalp. My eyes unwillingly roll to the back of my head at how fucking good that feels. "What are you, and why can't you be compelled?"

Compelled? Right. Like in vampire movies.

Oh, God. I'm going to die tonight.

I slap Millie's hand away. "I'm human!"

She narrows her eyes at me, and I squirm in my seat. Fuck, why does she have to be devastatingly gorgeous?

"*You* tell *me* what the fuck you are," I growl.

God, what am I even saying? Am I really asking someone if they're an undead creature of the night?

I've lost my mind.

But I need an answer.

I cross my arms over my chest and Millie's eyes fall to my forearms. Whatever she sees causes her pupils to expand.

That's how her eyes looked during sex.

Is that what happens when she's turned on? Her eyes turn black?

"Yes. We are vampires."

"Mills," the other woman hisses.

"It's fine, Layla. He's figured it out, and he can't be compelled so we might as well confess."

"Or we could kill him."

I blink and Millie has this Layla woman by the neck, up against a wall.

"You will not touch a hair on his head. He. Is. Mine."

"Jesus, Millie. I'm joking," Layla wheezes.

"Apologize. Now," Millie growls.

"I'm sorry," the other woman says, almost amused.

"I'm sorry what?"

"I'm sorry, Your Majesty."

The two stare into each other's eyes for a few more seconds before Millie releases her.

I stand and hold up my hands.

"Nope. I'm out."

I try to leave but barely make it two steps before Millie is in front of me.

"Wait, Teddy. I'm sorry. I can explain."

"*He is mine? Your Majesty?* I don't know what I walked in on here, but I'm freaked out, and I want to leave."

If I refuse her, will she kill me? She did just protect me from this other vampire.

My stomach twists because my brain wants to leave, but my body is begging me to stay. It wants to be near

Millie. My cock presses against my jeans because what she just did, slamming that woman up against the wall within milliseconds, was sexy as hell.

Which terrifies me because I should *not* find violence and threats of murder sexy.

"Please. Let me explain."

Something about the way Millie pleads for me gives me pause. Concern fills her face.

"Why me? Why do you care?"

She flinches. "What?"

"This is a one-night stand. We agreed it would be just sex. Well, we fucked. Now it's over."

"It doesn't have to be—"

"You lied to me!"

She shakes her head. "I didn't... Teddy."

She reaches for me, but I pull away. Her arm drops to her side, and she sighs.

"What would you have done outside that bar if I told you I was a vampire? Or if I waited and told you once I brought you back here?"

I grind my teeth because I know where this is going.

"You would have thought me mad and left. Am I right?"

I look away because she's absolutely right.

Except... I'm still here.

"But now I know, Millie, and it's... crazy. Vampires aren't supposed to be real."

"Would you like to see my fangs? Will that convince you?" She takes a knife from the holster of the woman standing next to her. "Or should I slice my arm and let you watch it heal before your eyes?"

Her friend—I assume she's Millie's friend—snatches the knife and secures it back in the holster. She regards Millie like she's lost her mind.

At least I'm not the only one.

"It's not that I don't believe you, Millie. I do. Which I can't explain and it's confusing, and I'm terrified, and I lied earlier because I actually hate being scared, and I just..."

I huff and run my hands through my hair. I want to leave. I want to run far away. At the same time, I desperately want to bring Millie into my arms and kiss her until her knees become weak. I *want* her to drink my blood.

Would she fuck me while sucking on my neck?

I need more booze. Something harder than beer. I turn away from the vamps and walk to a bar cart I remember seeing while scoping out the place. It's tucked between the kitchen and dining area.

I grab a bottle of whiskey, pour it in a glass, and chug it in three large gulps. The liquid coats my throat, warming my chest and sinking to my uneasy stomach.

This is just what I need right now. A fucking vampire crush. I wonder how old she is. Her *real* age. Vampires are immortal right?

Wait.

WAIT.

I have an idea.

Chapter 7 - Millie

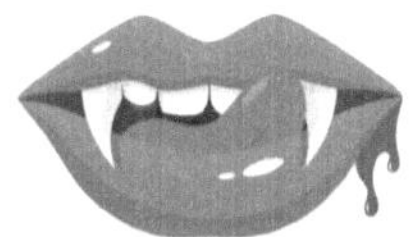

"Okay. I'll stay," Teddy says, and I let out one long breath of relief. Not that I need to breathe to live. I don't, but I still do it out of habit.

Why am I fighting for him to stay, though? I literally tried to compel him minutes ago. If it had worked, he'd be out of my life for good. Plus, he's right. We agreed tonight was just sex, a one-night stand. But my stomach aches and my chest grows heavy at the thought of him leaving me.

My whiplash emotions are about to give me a panic attack. Is that what's happening to me? A panic attack?

I know it's impossible since I have no heartbeat so it must be a phantom panic attack. Do those exist?

"What... what changed your mind?"

He shrugs. "I told you. My middle name is adventure."

I laugh. *Laugh!* That rarely happens. Layla regards me as if I've lost the plot.

I should apologize to her. I attacked her. I was... protective. I've *never* acted that way over anyone, especially a human.

"And you think you'll find adventure with me by staying?"

"You two did say there's a feral vampire on the loose. Are you going to go hunt them down? Can I go?"

Shit. That's right. I already forgot. That's why Layla is here.

"You want to go feral vampire hunting after admitting you lied about loving to be scared?"

He shrugs.

"Clearly staying with you means I'll be protected. No need to be scared. Also, did she refer to you as 'Your Majesty' earlier? Are you really a queen? I know I said you looked like one, but are you? Really?"

"Um..."

Before I can answer Teddy, Layla appears by my side. "Can I talk with you a moment?"

She drags me away and tosses me into a guest bedroom.

I listen to Teddy in the living room to make sure he's not leaving. He's at the bar again, pouring more liquor. He better not get wasted. I cannot deal with a drunk human right now.

"You tried to kill me!" Layla hisses. "Over a human?"

I scoff. "I did not try to kill you. I was merely warning you—"

I gasp.

"Yeah, you figured it out, didn't you?"

"There's no way." I start pacing the room.

"Your extreme attraction to this man? Territorial behavior over him?" Layla pauses, hesitant to say her next words. "His blood smells unlike anything I've ever encountered, Millie."

I fist my hands and stifle a growl.

Fuck! No. Stop it, Millie! Don't attack your best friend again.

"It sounds like he could be a blood mate. And since I'm not drooling over every little thing he does, I'm guessing he's yours."

"He can't be, though. I mean, can he?" I don't give Layla time to answer. She knows this is how I work through any problem I face. Pacing the floor and thinking out loud. "Blood mates are *rare*! I know of only two vampires in my five hundred years of living who've met their blood mate."

Blood mates are similar to fated mates, which is what gargoyles and shifters have. Many supernatural beings are destined to be with the ones who claim their souls. But vampires don't have souls. It's part of the curse against us. A curse that no one knows exactly how it came to be.

There have been theories over the years. A man broke a witch's heart so she used her magic to sentence him to an eternity of no daylight, no heartbeat, a thirst for blood, and no *love*.

Another I've heard is the original vampire emerged from hell, starved for blood, and infected humans with damnation and immortality, effectively turning them into creatures of the night.

Whatever the reason, we were created to lust not love. We desire blood and sex, not eternal companionship that's sweet and loving.

But if a vampire finds their *blood mate* and turns them, our curse is... changed. We are still vampires and drink blood to survive, but our heart restarts. We can withstand the sun's rays. We can *live* without living.

We can truly *love*.

It's as if the blood mate gives up a part of their soul. They become immortal and are bonded for life. A connection stronger than that of a sire.

A vampire with a blood mate is highly protective of them. It's why the two vampires who've successfully turned their mates have gone into hiding.

I say successfully because blood mates amongst vampires rarely survive. Many who meet their blood mate become addicted to their blood, and they're not able to control themselves during the first feeding and drain their mate dry.

A result of our curse and the evil festering inside us.

I've only had a taste of Teddy's blood and it was unlike anything I've ever had.

What would happen if he lets me drink from him? Would I be able to control myself? I wouldn't be able to live with myself if I killed him.

I shake my head. "This isn't supposed to happen. I had plans."

I desperately want to cry, but I avoid doing so since my tears turn to blood.

If Teddy is your blood mate, your tears would return to normal.

"What plans? Millie, you're not making sense."

"It doesn't matter. I can't deal with this possible blood mate shit right now." I rub my hands over my face and sigh. "How many bodies from the FV?" *Feral vamp.*

Layla doesn't answer right away, perhaps considering pushing me about Teddy and our connection, but after studying my face for a few minutes, she relents.

Did she see my vulnerability trying to break through? My fear?

I typically hide these emotions well, but tonight has been a struggle.

"Five and that's just in the past forty-eight hours."

"Fuck. That's a lot." I tap my finger on my lip, running through our options. "Okay. Call a council meeting for tomorrow night so we can discuss a plan of capture."

There goes my plan to face the sun. It's fine. I can do it anytime. Though I worry the longer I'm around Teddy, the more I'll want to stay.

"In the meantime, reach out to the gargoyles and ask them to add extra patrols around the city."

Layla taps away at her phone, then stuffs it in her jeans. "Done."

"Okay... You may go now."

Layla lingers, a stupid grin on her face.

"Just say it."

"What are you going to do about the pup?"

"I don't know. Send him away."

Layla snorts. "You know you won't be able to. Actually, you shouldn't be making official decisions right now if he is your mate. You're not thinking clearly."

Layla is right, and she smirks because she knows that I know she's right. Because she's a beautiful genius.

"Are you sure you don't want me to kill—"

"Do not finish that sentence unless you want me to tear out your heart."

She snorts, the hag. Layla likes to push my buttons and joke, but I do not find her funny.

At least, I'd never admit to her that I find her funny.

"So protective of your puppy, aren't you? I've missed this side of you. Violent and mean. It's why they named you queen, you know."

"Which was the biggest mistake the council has ever made. I didn't want it then, and I don't want it now."

I accepted the role because I thought it might have brought a little excitement to my life. I was wrong.

We return to the kitchen and find Teddy in my living room, staring at an original Rembrandt with his drink in one hand and an inquiring look on his face.

"I'm guessing you didn't buy this recently from a gallery or from an art dealer."

"You'd be correct," I say and lean my hip against the kitchen island, arms crossed.

"Nice to meet you, Puppy!" Layla yells as she exits the penthouse.

"Puppy?"

"Don't mind her."

He gives the oil painting of an old man praying one more glance before turning to me. "Did he give that to you personally?"

"I *bought* it from him personally."

I just realized that Teddy changed the record to Etta James. *A Sunday Kind Of Love* plays and it's the only sound in the apartment. The song is romantic... Sensual.

He walks to where I stand, setting his drink down and holding out his hand. "You owe me a dance."

"I don't think now is the time—"

"Come dance with me, Millie." His demanding tone lights up my body.

How can this mere human make me melt into a puddle?

I take his hand and he leads me to the center of the living room. He snakes his arm around my waist and tugs me to his body. We take small steps, slowly turning in circles while swaying to the smooth notes. I can't help leaning my head on Teddy's shoulder.

Because he's being so kind and gentle with me despite learning I'm a cold-blooded killer.

"Tell me everything," he says, his breath fanning the top of my head. "Starting with how old you are."

"I'm... 500 years old."

He sucks in a sharp breath.

"I was turned when I was thirty. A vampire named Henry. He was going to kill my family, and I begged him to take me instead. Spare their lives, and in turn, he gets mine. A vow for the vamp, offering my soul."

Teddy's palm slides up and down my back, soothing me. Encouraging me to continue.

"He turned me. Then..."

My voice breaks. We stop dancing and Teddy pulls back. He cups my cheek.

"What is it, Milli Vanilli?"

The silly nickname makes me smile because it's cheesy, but it's mine, and I've never had a silly nickname before.

Teddy's bright and accepting self has somehow relaxed me, and I'm able to confess the worst thing I've ever done.

"He forced me to kill my own family."

Teddy immediately brings me in for a hug, and the move surprises me because I can't remember the last time someone held me like this and consoled me, allowing me to just... *feel*. I start crying, sobbing into his chest and not even caring that he'll see the horror of my blood-stained cheeks after. I shake against his body, my eyes aching and my throat tightening. He kisses the top of my head and rubs his palm over my back.

"I hated him," I continue, still nuzzled against my sunshine man. I'm bleeding all over the Milli Vanilli shirt.

Still, I don't care. Not when he's treating me with such compassion. "The moment he sired me, my life belonged to him. He could control me. Force me to do his bidding. For the first three hundred years of my vampire life, I killed. I tortured. And I enjoyed it."

I peel myself out of Teddy's hold and step back.

"I'm a monster." I point at my face.

He stares back with soft eyes. No fear. No judgment. *He's too good for me.*

I turn away from him, but he comes up behind me, placing his hands on my shoulders. He smooths them down my arms and then back up before moving a piece of hair out of the way.

"That's not who you are anymore."

His lips press against my neck, and I lean into him. His nearness is comforting. He's letting me know that I won't scare him away.

"No. It's not who I am anymore, but I can never forgive myself for the things I've done."

I pause because I hate talking about this part of my life. I *never* talk about this part of my life. Only Layla knows the things I have done.

"Tell me more."

Such a gentle command.

This man, this *human,* makes me want to share every-thing with him.

"When I arrived in New York City in the 1800s, my reputation followed. I was approached by some elder vampires. They were part of an organization called WOVE or World Organization of Vampire Elites. They wanted to form a council and implement rules for our kind. They sought me out to serve on it, and I did because it was about time vampires had rules to follow in order to live in this human world.

"Up until then, we could kill as we pleased and turn any human we wanted. But people were noticing and with technology rapidly advancing, rumors spread quickly. Fear was rampant. We had to protect ourselves because the humans formed teams of hunters to find and kill us."

Teddy places another kiss on my neck, and I close my eyes. Every time he touches me, a thrill shoots between my legs.

"What are the rules?"

"No feeding in public, violators have their fangs ripped out." He sucks in a sharp breath. "It's painful, but they grow back after a few weeks."

"What else?"

"No turning a human unless given approval by the council. If a vampire were to break this rule, both sire and newborn vamp are killed."

"That's harsh," Teddy says and spins me back around to continue dancing.

"We have to control the vampire population. If too many humans die, we run out of food. If too many are turned, we run out of food. We have synthetic blood, but it's only for emergency situations. It's not sustainable."

The song is coming to an end and Teddy dips me. I yelp. Then I *laugh*.

Not the first time he's made me feel joy.

And I love it so much.

He tugs me upright and kisses me, first on the lips, then along my blood-streaked tears. I gasp when his tongue laps up the mess. He hums the moment the blood hits his taste buds. It takes him a couple minutes to clean it all before he pulls back with a goofy smile.

God, he's too cute.

"This feral vampire," he begins. "What will happen to them?"

"They will be caught and killed. They broke our number one rule. No killing humans. This vampire is putting our existence at risk of discovery. We have vampires embedded with the NYPD so we can clean up these murders and compel humans who were witnesses, but there's always a chance someone will be missed and with cellphones in every hand..."

A new Etta James song plays, *I Just Want To Make Love To You,* and Teddy's palm returns to the small of my back, the other cupping my hand. Before tonight, it's been decades since I've danced with anyone. Perhaps longer. Mostly because I'm not a fan of dancing. I have two left feet that refuse to find the beat.

But I love dancing with Teddy.

"Are there rules about compelling?"

"Yes. No compelling for sexual pleasure. No compelling a human to commit a crime. And no repeat compelling as it could cause brain damage."

"You said you tried to compel me, but it didn't work."

I peel myself from his grip and drop my arms.

"About that..."

Before I can explain, my cellphone rings.

The pizza is here.

Chapter 8 - Teddy

Millie tips the pizza delivery worker well and closes the door.

"Can you even eat this?" I ask as she sets the box on the kitchen island.

She frowns. "No, but I enjoy the smell."

"So you only drink blood? Like, from a living person?"

"That *is* how vampirism works."

She grabs me a plate, places two slices on it, and scoots it to me. Then she pours herself a glass of wine. I gulp back my third glass of whiskey and stand to get my fourth.

I wobble and Millie is at my side in an instant.

"Jesus, Millie!" I grab my chest as my heart lurches. It's the second time she's snuck up on me. "My mind can't comprehend you being that freakishly fast."

She smirks, not at all sorry. "Are you okay?"

She places her cold hand on my forearm and the other on my shoulder to steady me. I hate how my stomach dips and my cock twitches at her touch. Her eyes darken as she glances at my mouth. My heart beats faster, remembering the kisses we've shared. How *hungry* we were for each other. How she let me take control and claim her.

I still want that.

She places her palm over my chest.

"Is this beating faster for me?"

I clear the lust from my throat because while I want nothing more than to ravish this woman again, I still have questions.

Also, I might be a little drunk. I can hold my liquor, but I've had three full glasses of top-shelf whiskey. Plus, I haven't eaten since lunch.

But what's strange? My body is buzzing. I almost feel high. The colors around Millie's penthouse pop out. The music from the record player is crisp. The pizza smells as if it was cooked here instead of down the street.

"I think I need to drink some water."

Millie moves to the row of cabinets in a blur, faster than my eyes can follow. She grabs a glass and fills it with ice and water from the dispenser on the front of the fridge.

All within ten seconds flat.

Ugh. Fine. It's fucking awesome she can do that.

"Tell me about how you became queen," I say when she places the water in front of me. "Is that why those men in suits were down in your lobby and out in front of your penthouse?"

"I'll tell you what," she begins. "For every part of my life I share with you, you have to share a part of your life with me."

"Fair enough."

"And you owe me a story."

"Technically, we're even because I told you about my parents being controlling, which caused my need for control in the bedroom."

"But I shared how I became a vampire *and* told you how I ended up here in NYC. I've covered more years. You owe me more stories."

"It's not a competition, Mildred."

She scrunches up her nose at me using her full name. "Fine, you brat."

Does she realize how adorable she is when her button nose does that? Like an adorable little bunny. Probably not the best way to describe a dangerous vampire, but she *is* cute.

Gorgeous.

Stunning.

"Yes. Those men you saw are my guards. They go where I go but when we met tonight, I had snuck out because sometimes I want to be alone. As for how I became queen? I told you about the council, right?"

I nod.

"Well, they needed a leader, and they all nominated me because of my ruthless reputation. Over the years, the vampires in this city and all the other supernatural beings started calling me the vampire queen. Therefore, I am. Now, every major city has a king or queen."

"Wait, wait, wait... there are other supernatural beings? What do you mean? Like, werewolves and shit?"

"Yes."

"What else?"

"Your pizza is getting cold."

"What else, Millie?"

She sighs. "Gargoyles, demons, angels, sirens, shifters, mothmen—"

"No fucking way."

She pushes my plate closer to me, and I finally pick up a slice and take a bite.

I groan because this is damn good pizza.

"Your turn," Millie says, taking advantage of me with my mouth full to play our little game. "Tell me about your childhood. Anything unusual happen to you? Your parents... are you sure they're human and not, say, witches?"

"Witches?!" I ask around the food.

"Yes, they're real too."

I shake my head and swallow my bite. "No. My dad is an accountant, and my mom is a teacher. Not exactly magical career paths."

"You'd be surprised."

"No. Nothing unusual. I promise. Why are you asking though? Is it because you can't hypnotize me?"

"It's called compelling and yes."

I wonder if that has anything to do with my...

I shake the thought from my head. It won't matter unless I can convince her to—

"I want you to bite me."

She nearly spits out the mouthful of wine she just drank.

"I want to know what it feels like."

Millie smirks and gently places the wineglass down on the marble countertop.

"I don't think you're ready for that."

"What do you mean?"

"Well, when I... feed from someone, *I'm* the one in control."

She slowly walks around the corner of the kitchen island. I turn in my seat and spread my legs. She saunters right between them.

A perfect fit.

My palms slide around to her backside, and I squeeze handfuls of her ass. She drapes her arms over my shoulders.

"Would you give me control, Puppy?"

Puppy.

So it's a nickname. I hate it.

I love it.

Maybe even more than when she calls me Theodore.

I nod, letting out a shaky breath because now that I know Millie is a *vampire*, she has all the power. She could kill me with her bare hands. She could suck the life out of me, and I'd thank her in the afterlife.

She grabs my hard cock through my jeans and squeezes.

"Would you let me tie you up? Blindfold you?"

My dick jerks in her hold. "Yes, I'd… I'd like that."

Her nipples poke through her top so I lean in and take one in my mouth through the fabric. She moans, her head falling back.

I lift the shirt for better access. She's not wearing a bra. My lips wrap around the peak of her breast, and I lap my tongue over the nipple. Her hands bury into my hair and tug.

While my mouth and fingertips work her tit, I slide my other hand down her front and behind the band of her sweats. My fingers find her soaked pussy. I sink them inside and she groans, clutching onto my shoulders for support.

"If you're technically dead," I say and start pumping. "How do you get wet like this? I thought you had to have a heartbeat to pump blood down there or something."

My thumb presses against her clit, and I cover her nipple with my mouth again. This time I drag my teeth over it. Her pussy responds by choking my fingers.

"It's... it's..." She's whimpering and I smirk, loving how I can make her fall apart with just my touch.

For a woman who claims she loves control, she's quick to give it all to me.

I remove my fingers and stand suddenly, lifting my hand to my mouth and sucking off her pleasure.

Her fangs fall down at the move. Once I've had every delectable drop, I cup her face and pull her close so I can lick her mouth.

"Can you taste yourself?"

"Yes."

My tongue swipes over the points of her fangs and she moans.

"I want you to taste me. Take control of me. Drink my blood. Take all of it if you want."

"What? No, I won't take all your blood. You'd die."

I want her to turn me.

I lift her off the ground and she yelps before I lay her back on the kitchen island counter. The move knocks over her wineglass and the pizza box falls to the ground.

"Teddy!"

"I'll clean it up later," I say and tug her sweats down. "I want something sweet to eat first."

I don't give her time to respond and wrap my arms around her thick thighs to bury my face in her cunt. I lap my tongue over her clit and suck it into my mouth. She moans and grabs hold of my hair.

I spread her pussy lips apart and thrust my tongue inside her, pumping in and out while I massage her clit with my thumb.

"Yes, Teddy. Go faster, harder."

My vampy babe loves it rough.

I replace my tongue with two fingers and drive them in and out while I suck her clit, listening to her reactions as guidance.

It doesn't take long to get her worked up. Her body tenses, her walls clamp down, then she's moaning and shaking with an orgasm.

I love how vocal she is... how I make her scream.

She lies there in orgasmic bliss, but I'm not done. I take her hand and pull. She hops off the counter, and I lead us to her bedroom.

"You're such a good girl, coming for me."

I have no clue where her bedroom is, so I keep walking down the long hallway until she points me to a back room.

"I want you to give me another orgasm."

I open the door and find a massive room nearly the size of my studio apartment. The bed is a king, with black bedding. The black walls are decorated with green vines and fairy lights snaking throughout. A vanity sits along one wall next to a black couch and matching chair.

Yep. This is Millie's bedroom.

"But there's just one rule," I continue.

"And what would that be?" she asks, crossing her arms while she watches me strip out of my T-shirt and jeans.

"You don't get to come until you bite me."

She narrows her silver eyes at me.

"Why are you so adamant about me biting you?"

I drop my briefs and my cock springs out. Her eyes fall to it, and she bares her fangs.

Fuck, that's sexy.

"Because your fangs are out, and I know you've been holding back. Why? Do you not drink from the people you fuck?"

She shifts on her feet. "I do, but…"

"Exactly. I want this, and I know you do too. If there's a reason you're hesitating, then tell me. Are you worried you'll scare me away? Because after everything you've shared, I'm still here."

I grab the hair at her nape and tilt her head back so I can kiss her. The kiss is rough, and my bottom lip drags across her fangs, hard enough I start bleeding.

I deepen the kiss, and she greedily sucks on my bleeding lip, making sure to take every last drop.

With my free hand, I cup her pussy and sink a finger inside. I pump it casually, opposite of the fevered kiss we share. Her hands are all over the place. One is buried in my hair and the other slides down my body, over my meaty chest and soft stomach until grabbing my hard cock. She fists my shaft up and down, matching my movements and squeezing to add just enough pressure.

She ends the kiss and pushes my chest, forcing me to fall onto the bed. A chill washes over my body as I watch her grin transform.

The predator has trapped the prey.

"Fine. You want me to bite you?"

I nod, a little too excitedly, and her eyes fall to my cock as it jerks and leaks precum.

She walks into her closet and returns seconds later with cuffs, a blindfold, and a knife. My eyes widen. The knife should scare me, but instead, my dick gets harder.

"I told you I take control when I feed and you've been a real brat tonight, Mr. Thibodeaux."

She's at the side of the bed and reaches out for my hand.

"Are you sure this is what you want?"

I have a feeling she never asks and just *takes*, but she knows how much it means to me. Her asking to take control means she respects me.

"Please. Take it."

Chapter 9 - Millie

What am I doing?

This is a bad idea.

What if I drain him? Kill him? His blood is too potent, addictive. I've only had a taste, and it was heavenly. If he really is my blood mate, that would explain why it tastes so good.

Up until now, I've managed not to rip his throat out and take it all.

Maybe he should be the one cuffing me to the bed. Keep my hands secured so I can't hold onto him while I drink. But that would leave me vulnerable. I've heard stories of vampires who relented control only to be staked mid-sex or mid-bite.

I can do this. I'll be able to stop myself.

"Do you trust me?"

"Yes."

"You should never trust a vampire."

He laughs nervously, despite the warning being true.

I take his hand and cuff it to the bedframe, then I climb onto the bed and straddle him to secure his other hand.

"I'm going to blindfold you now. Okay? I want you to rely on your other senses for this."

Teddy swallows hard, his heart pounds against his chest.

"Don't be *scared*," I say, teasing him about his earlier confession.

"It freaks me out that you can hear my heart. Vampire hearing is really that good?"

I lean in and lick his lips.

"Yes, and I'm going to need you to calm down."

Adrenaline filled blood tastes the best. Aroused blood even better.

He's both.

Mix that with him possibly being my blood mate? Yeah, this is not a good idea.

I'm going to devour him.

"What? Why does your face look like that? Have you changed your mind?"

Okay, you'd think I'd have better control over my facial expressions after all these years. Am I letting my guard down because of Teddy? Because there's something about him that feels... right?

Because he could be my mate?

Still, I hesitate to trust a human I've only known for hours. I may want my life to end, but I will die on my terms.

I take the blindfold and cover his eyes. He sucks in sharply.

"But what if I want to see you?"

I should get tape for his mouth. My adorable little chatterbox.

"No talking."

A smile spreads across his face at the order, which mirrors what he said to me earlier.

He lets out a shuddering breath when I gently place my lips over his. He tries to slip his tongue past them, but I'm already moving my mouth to his jaw for another soft kiss.

Once I reach his neck, I scrape my fangs over the skin and he moans, his cock jerking underneath me. I move my hips in small circles, sliding my slickness over his shaft.

"Millie," he groans.

I pinch and twist his nipples, causing him to buck.

"No talking."

He opens his mouth to defy me but decides against it, clamping his jaw tight.

"Feel my touch." My palms smooth over his chest and stomach, his body tensing at the icy strokes. "Listen." I sink my fingers into my pussy, thrusting them in and out. "Can you hear how wet I am for you?" Upon removing them, I bring them up to his nose. "Smell me."

He sniffs and his cock jumps again.

"Taste me." I shove the fingers into his mouth, and he licks them frantically.

I adjust myself so I can grab his dick with my free hand and sink down his shaft. He moans around my fingers, then sucks them harder. I start riding him and he tugs on the cuffs, desperate to touch me. He hisses as the metal digs into his wrists.

"You're being such a good little puppy," I whisper, removing my fingers from his mouth to bury them in his hair and tug his head back.

My fangs ache with how badly I want to drink from him. I scrape them over the skin of his neck again and he responds by jerking his hips up into me. My pussy throbs around him and my head falls back in complete euphoria.

I'm not going to last long, and I'm guessing neither will he.

I rip the blindfold off. He takes in my black eyes and my fangs peeking out past my lips. He tries to lean in to kiss me, but I tug on his hair again, jerking his head back.

"Look up Teddy."

He swallows hard, and I watch his Adam's apple bob.

"You have a mirror over your bed?"

I'm slowly fucking him, trying to pace myself.

"Yes, and I want you to watch."

"Watch you bite me?"

"Watch me *feed* from you. Here."

I stop moving and within a blink of an eye, I've broken one of the cuffs to free one of his hands. I grab the knife I set aside and place it in his palm.

"If I don't stop, stab me with this. It doesn't matter where."

"What? No!"

He tries to give it back to me, but I wrap my hand over his, securing the handle in his fist and press it against his chest.

"You won't kill me, but this will incapacitate me enough to stop me from draining you of life."

He stares into my eyes, and I can see him thinking.

"What if I want..."

"Teddy, no." He clamps his mouth shut, the muscles in his jaw rippling. "That's not how it works. Me draining you of blood means you die, and you *don't* come back as a vampire. Turning a human is a process, one I'm not prepared for. Besides, I don't turn people."

"Ever?"

"Ever."

"Why?"

I start bouncing on his cock again, and he groans. Good. Now is not the time to talk about this.

"Just... hold on to the knife and use it if I can't control myself."

"Why wouldn't you be able to control yourself?"

"Because there's something special about your blood."

I don't give him time to respond and sink my teeth into his neck.

Chapter 10 - Teddy

I scream in pain, jolting underneath her.

That pain quickly turns to pleasure.

My cock grows harder as she draws my blood into her mouth, gulping it down as if she's tasting human life for the first time. My head tilts back in ecstasy, my eyelids fluttering as they struggle to stay open.

Watch me feed from you.

The mirror.

I force my eyes back open and spot us on the bed, Millie fucking me wildly with her head latched to my neck.

Holy shit, this is hot.

I plant my feet on the bed and drop the knife to wrap my free arm around Millie's waist for leverage as I meet her thrusts with my own. I watch us, giving ourselves to each other. Millie taking *my* life to satiate her hunger.

Her cunt squeezes my cock as she gets close to coming and it sends me over the edge. I moan out my release, splattering her walls with my cum.

But she doesn't stop drinking.

My eyes start to droop, my vision blurry.

There's something special about your blood.

"Millie," I say, but my voice is weak, and she doesn't seem to hear it.

I grab her long hair and tug, causing her to growl against my neck.

Hold on to the knife and use it if I can't control myself.

I feel around the mattress for where I dropped the weapon. My pulse slows, and I'm seconds from passing out when my fingers brush against cold metal. I find the handle and pick it up.

Millie unlatches from my neck, but it's too late. I'm already plunging the knife into her side.

She screams in pain and jumps off me.

I pass out.

I wake in a dark room, naked and no longer cuffed to the bed. My head throbs and my neck aches.

The moment I graze my fingertips over the spot where Millie bit me, I moan and a chill ripples through my body. My cock jerks, remembering her sweet cunt choking me as she drank from me. How I came inside her while she drained me of life.

Then she took too much. She said that could happen. Except... she let me go, and I still stabbed her.

I feel around in the dark for my phone or anything to give me light. My hand bumps into the bedside table and then the base of a lamp. My eyes burn when I click it on. I rub my hands over my face and once my vision adjusts, I turn my head and nearly have a heart attack.

"Goddamn it, Millie. You really have to stop appearing out of nowhere. It's creepy how quiet and fast you move."

She's sitting on the bed next to me and smiles. "I'm sorry. I thought you heard me come in."

"If you wanted me to know you were here, you would have turned on a light."

She laughs, and it's such a delicate sound coming from an intimidating, powerful, and bloodthirsty vampire.

"Ok fine, you caught me. I was watching you sleep."

"For how long?"

"You've been passed out for about half an hour. I came in to check on you five minutes ago. Did you know you look like a Victorian child dying of the plague when you sleep?"

"Show me. What did I look like?"

She curls her arms against her chest, wrists limp, and throws her head back, opening her mouth.

I bark out a laugh; one because she actually showed me, and two because that's exactly how I look when I sleep. My college friends always made fun of me for it. They'd snap pictures while I slept and tease me about it when I'd wake up.

Pain rips through my head and I grab my temples. Okay, no laughing after being nearly drained of blood.

"See. That's why I didn't turn on the light. I knew you'd wake up with a headache. Here."

She picks up two pills from the bedside table and places them in my palm. I don't even question what they are and pop them in my mouth, chasing them with the glass of water she hands me.

Once I set the empty glass down, I let my eyes travel over her body. She's in a robe and her hair is wet. I inhale her sweet floral smell and my cock hardens. Her enhanced vampire vision notices and her silver eyes fall to my groin.

Wait.

I did stab her, right? Or was it a dream?

I push the fabric of her robe away, revealing her naked body underneath.

"Teddy," she warns, lust captivating her voice.

But I don't stop. My fingertips trace over her sides, looking for the wound.

"Didn't I..."

"Stab me? Yes, but I'm a vampire. I heal fast."

My eyes jerk up to hers. "Can becoming a vampire fix other things? Like medical things?"

"Being a vampire doesn't fix anything."

She stands and walks to the dresser, grabbing a stack of clothes sitting on top. She hands me a black Rolling Stones T-shirt, black jeans, and boxer briefs, then steps back and crosses her arms.

"What if your blood could save lives?"

"That's not how it works—"

"Save me."

Her head jerks as if she's been slapped.

"What?"

"Save me, Millie. I'm dying. I found out today. Well," I glance at the clock on the bedside table, "yesterday now that it's past midnight."

"I told you that's not how it works," her voice is barely a whisper, but the room is quiet enough I hear every word.

"Then explain it."

"Our blood isn't a miracle cure. It doesn't heal anything. *I'm* able to use it to heal bite wounds to keep our existence a secret, but that's it."

"But if you were to turn me..."

"If we saved every terminally ill person, the world would be overrun with vampires. We'd have no food. The human race would end."

Her words sting because I'd expected her to want to save me... to be with me. For what? Eternity? The thought is insane. I've known this woman for less than a day.

Then why does it feel as if it's been a lifetime?

"How long do you have?" she asks, her voice softening and full of compassion.

The vamp has a heart after all.

"Four months."

"Cancer?"

"Inoperable brain tumor—" My voice cracks and pressure builds behind my eyes.

I start crying.

It's the first time since finding out that I've let myself *feel.*

"Teddy," she says, returning to the side of the bed. She stands in front of me, and I bury my head into her bare stomach because she hasn't pulled her robe closed. "Did you get a second opinion?"

"I got three." I wrap my arms around her waist and sob. "I don't want to die."

Her fingers comb through my hair and her touch sends a wave of comfort through my body.

I don't understand that. Any of this.

She's a stranger, yet she feels like my soulmate.

I have a million questions. Like why am I special? Why is my *blood* special? I open my mouth to start asking, but Millie cuts me off.

"I have an idea," she says, pulling away from me. "Get dressed. We're going out."

Out?

Before I can ask her where or what we're doing, she's out of the room.

Vampire speed.

Chapter 11 - Millie

We're in the backseat of an SUV, heading to Lower Manhattan.

My leg shakes and I chew on my nails.

I'm *nervous*.

And confused.

I'm feeling a lot of emotions that I've managed to keep locked deep down in the pits of my nonexistent soul.

I *like* this man. He makes me giddy and happy.

Happy.

I haven't been happy since before Henry when I had a pulse, a husband, and two children.

I know the blood mate bond is fueling these emotions. I need to speak with the vampires who've met their mates.

What did they experience? Was it this intense emotionally *and* physically?

Or maybe it's just Teddy. He's handsome, funny, smart.

And he's dying.

Fuck!

This is not what I had planned! I was going to end my existence at sunrise. Now I'm considering living and turning this man to save him... to have him by my side for eternity.

I've never needed to rely on another person. Even when Layla and I were together, we were both independent. We cared for each other but needed our space. And Henry forced me to rely on him, despite me being the one covering up his massacres. I saved him from angry pitchfork carrying mobs far too many times.

The asshole.

I startle when Teddy pulls my hand away from my mouth and weaves his fingers with mine.

He doesn't say anything. Doesn't ask me what's wrong or try to reassure me.

God, why do I love that so much?

But I should have known the silence wouldn't last. The happy chatterbox man's curiosity gets the best of him.

"Does garlic harm you?"

I was wondering when he'd ask these questions. Most humans ask the same ones when discovering we exist. Urban legends and mainstream media got some of it right.

I sigh. "There's nothing special about garlic except that it smells wretched and gives humans bad breath."

"And I thought vampires weren't supposed to have a reflection, but tonight, when we fucked... you did."

"That one is a myth. I've always had a reflection."

"You can't turn into a bat, can you?"

I don't even entertain that question.

"Your silence must mean no."

"Anything else you want to know?"

His eyes trail down my body, ending on my crotch.

"How do you get wet for sex if you have no heartbeat for blood flow?"

I shrug. "We're not entirely sure. Despite not having a heartbeat, we still walk and talk and use our brains. Blood is our life sustenance. Perhaps it is the blood that fuels our arousal as well."

He nods, being his usual accepting self.

"So you don't sleep in a coffin?"

"Not anymore. Technology is fascinating and now we have UV guards on windows and have no need to hide in coffins."

The drive from Midtown doesn't take long since it's in the middle of the night and traffic is sparse. Before Teddy can ask any more questions, the driver is pulling up to CBGB on Bowery.

"I haven't been here yet!" Teddy says, his face lighting up the moment he spots the legendary music club.

"It's just a clothing store now. There are some pieces of the club still left inside, but it's definitely not what it used to be."

My door opens and I get out with Teddy trailing behind. He spots my bodyguards and gives them a quick nod, smiling ear to ear.

Always smiling.

Even after telling me he's dying, he fails to let it stop him from living.

"Are they... also vampires?"

"No. They're griffins, but they're masked to appear human."

Teddy pauses and stares at the two large men who wear suits, sunglasses, and no emotions on their faces.

"Like, part lion, part bird?"

Wylan, the guard who has been with me for decades, scoffs. But to me, it sounded more like the angry call of an eagle.

"Lion's body and an eagle's head and wings. Don't call them birds. It's rude."

Teddy runs his hands through his hair.

"Shit. I'm sorry..." He leans in to me. "How do I gender them?"

"They are male."

He turns to them. "I'm so sorry, fellas. I'm just new to... all this. I'm learning and I promise I'll get it right next time."

He wants to learn?

Learn to be a part of my life?

Of course, because he's hoping I'll save him.

How could I not?

I shake the thought from my head and pull Teddy away from my guards, who at least appear impressed that Teddy is being so accepting of our world.

"Is this place open?"

"No. We're not going to CBGB."

I approach a side door and knock in the pattern that requests entry. It opens and a green-skinned demon appears in the entrance.

"Your Majesty," they say, a mischievous grin spreading across their face, flanking sharp fangs. They bow, but there's no need for that.

This demon is trying to get a rise out of me.

"Thalia."

"Holy shit," Teddy whispers beside me. Unlike my guards, Thalia is *not* masked.

"You haven't been here in decades. Welcome back," they goad. "And you've brought a human?"

The demon sniffs the air and their black eyes glow red.

"He smells fantastic."

Before this hellish fucker can finish their words, my fangs have dropped, and I've slammed my fist through their chest.

I pull out Thalia's heart and they fall to the ground.

"Millie! What the fuck?!" Teddy shrieks.

"It's fine. They're not dead. Demons are quite difficult to kill. This one's heart will regenerate within hours."

"Yet you know better than to attack my employees, Vampire Queen. Especially in front of humans."

"Vara," I say, smiling at the sphinx. "Perhaps your demons should keep their mouths shut when speaking about what's mine."

Vara's claws are out, fangs bared. She ruffles her feathered wings and whips her tail back and forth. Her mane of long blonde hair falls over her shoulders, enough to cover her bare, fur-covered chest.

She's nearly naked except for a thin layer of cloth to cover her cunt.

"Impressive. A human has enchanted the vamp. I'm eager to learn how that happened. In the meantime, I'll spread the word that he's off limits. But you know that may not be enough."

I cross my arms. "I know how it works but hearing it from you wouldn't hurt. Now, tell me what you want in return."

Vara shrugs her shoulders. "I think you know what I want."

"And you know it's the one thing I can't give you."

"We shall see."

Vara turns away and disappears into the dark hallway.

Another demon, this one appearing human but the smell of death on them tells me they're a reaper, replaces Thalia at the door.

"What does she want?" Teddy asks once we're inside.

"A date with Layla."

"Layla your friend? Who is a vampire? Do supernaturals date each other?" Teddy holds my hand tight as he follows me through the hallway, relying solely on my night vision. "What type of supernatural being is Vara?"

"Vara is a sphinx. Similar to a griffin, but with a human head. She's one of the few of her kind left. Decades ago, I granted her sanctuary in New York City from hunters wanting her feathers, which are made of gold. She's become quite the powerful supe since then. Owns most of the supernatural night clubs around the five boroughs. Well respected too."

We take a set of stairs, moving slowly to make sure Teddy doesn't trip and fall in the darkness and break his neck. I wouldn't be able to bring him back from that.

"And yes, we fuck and date a variety of supernaturals. I have an ex who's a gargoyle."

"What did you mean by your guards being masked to appear human? Is that, like, magic, or something?"

"That's exactly what it means. Over the years, many supernatural beings have evolved the ability to mask their natural form to blend in and appear human."

"That's badass."

We approach a door that has a light shining directly on the text painted on the metal.

"The 27 Club?" Teddy asks.

"The owner got the name idea after seeing a trend with celebrities dying at age twenty-seven. It's morbid, I know, but some of those musicians who died came back as the undead."

"No way! Which ones?"

"I've seen Janis Joplin, Jim Morrison, and Biggie perform here, but it's been years."

"Elvis?"

"Surprisingly, no. A few books and television shows have turned him into a vampire, but every human who becomes a vampire must be registered. Elvis is not on the list. Most of the celebrities who were turned were done so with pre-approval. They bought their immortality by funding our research."

"What research?"

"We have synthetic blood that we can drink to satiate hunger in an emergency situation. We're also working on a cure to vampirism; however, many believe we are the products of a curse, and the cure will never be found. If there was a cure, at least we'd have a choice. We could reduce the vampire population and make way for terminally ill people without threatening the end of humankind."

I open the door and music welcomes us. A smooth voice sings, accompanied by the notes of a keyboard and the beats of a drum set, filling the club with the sounds of my past.

"No way," Teddy whispers, his mouth hanging open, eyes wide. "That's Otis Redding. But he died in a plane crash."

"And he was saved by a vampire."

Technically, Redding's turning wasn't approved but the vampire who sired him was old and tired of living, so he gave his life so the R&B legend could become immortal.

WOVE granted the exception.

I could give my life for Teddy.

The thought quickly vanishes. If I had that choice earlier in the night, it would have been simple.

Now? Now I have hope and hope is intoxicating. It's motivating me to stay in this world.

Otis wraps up *(Sittin' On) the Dock of the Bay* and the crowd cheers and whistles.

"Do you want a drink?" I ask, leading us to a booth off to the side of the room.

The 27 Club isn't too large. There's a stage at the back and booths along the side walls. A bar sits along the fourth wall and an open space in the middle allows for dancing or crowds to stand and watch whichever band or musician is on stage.

The lights are low, only the ones highlighting the stage and the bar illuminate the space.

Supernatural vision doesn't require more.

"Any craft beer is fine. I'm not picky. I like trying new things too."

I wave over a waitress and order Teddy a Brooklyn-made beer and a glass of wine for me.

I try to ignore all the eyes on us. Teddy is oblivious as he nods his head to Otis performing *Love Man*. Every supernatural in the room gawks at the vampire queen entertaining a human.

I spot several demons and shifters, a couple fae, a handful of ghosts, one siren, a centaur, and several other vampires.

A high-ranking fae is the first one to approach us.

"Your Majesty," he says, his voice like a song. But his fae powers won't work on me.

Teddy, however, jerks his head at the sound of Korna's words.

"You haven't introduced us to your friend." He grins and his purple eyes glow.

Korna, like most fae, is gorgeous with dark black hair that he has cut short to his head to showcase his pointed ears. He's tall, slim, but toned.

"*He* is none of your business," I say at the same time Teddy holds out his hand, attempting to introduce himself.

I slap Teddy's offered greeting away seconds before Korna takes it.

"Never shake hands with fae, Teddy," I say to my supernatural clueless human, then turn my attention back to Korna. "And this one is mine, faerie. You will not touch him. Don't come near him. Don't even look at him."

He bristles at me calling him faerie. He is a faerie, but the word 'fairy' became popular with children's stories, and they all hate the reference, as it makes them appear cute and magical.

There's nothing cute about the fae. They are all cruel and manipulative.

"This one must be special. To have a queen's attention?" Korna leans in and inhales deeply in Teddy's direction. "We all just want to know—"

I have him by the neck and on the ground before he can finish the words.

"I *said*... Stay. Away."

Korna wraps his fingers around my wrists and an electric current zaps me. I grit my teeth at the pain, which should have knocked me out cold by now. My fangs—which I haven't sheathed since entering the club—pierce into my lips and draw blood.

"Queen Millie, release him. Lord Kornavian, stop electrocuting her," Vara says, appearing beside us.

Korna relents first and stands, brushing dirt off his tailored suit. He sneers at me.

"I don't know how you managed to tolerate my power, Queen." His eyes move to Teddy before returning to me. "He has every supernatural in here foaming at the mouth.

If I were you, *Mildred*, I'd claim him for all to see. Your words may not be enough."

Chapter 12 - Teddy

*C*laim him for all to see.

The tan man with dark hair and purple eyes, who is definitely not human, walks away. The waitress drops off our drinks, and I know beer won't be enough, so I order whiskey right before she leaves.

I chug down my beer, trying to understand what just happened.

"Teddy," Millie says, approaching the booth. "Are you okay?"

No, I don't think I'm okay at all. My life is weird as fuck right now, but I'm here in a supernatural night club where a strange man sniffed me and said I was special. Now Otis freaking Redding is playing *These Arms of Mine* and all I want to do is dance with the woman who not only terrifies me but also makes me feel whole.

It's as if I'd been searching for a lost item my entire life and have finally stumbled upon it. I don't understand it, and I need answers. Especially after what just happened.

I stand and reach out my hand. "Let's dance."

She hesitates but takes it.

"Teddy, we should talk—"

I drag her to the center of the dance floor and tug her body against mine, snaking my arm around her waist.

"Oh, we're going to talk, Milli Vanilli. But we're also going to dance because when will I ever get a chance to do this again?"

"Actually, Otis plays here often, so..."

I sigh, because she's trying to make a joke and it's kinda adorable, but I'm also mad at her.

Well, not so much mad but frustrated because she's been keeping things from me.

"What does it mean to claim me?"

"They just want to see me feed from you. I can say you are mine all I want, but to drink from you in front of everyone secures your safety. It's a rite of passage of sorts. No one will dare touch you."

"But you fed from me earlier. I still have the marks."

I graze my fingers over the spot, but I barely feel puncture marks.

"I used my blood to heal it. I wasn't sure if you would want them…" She looks away. "Drinking from you in private doesn't prove my protective claim over you. I have to do it around other supernatural beings. Almost like I'm a dog marking my territory."

Okay. I suppose that makes sense. Or doesn't.

"I thought one of the rules was no feeding in public?"

"This is a private establishment for supernaturals. It's considered neutral territory. We can feed if given permission. Or if it is to claim a human to protect them."

The idea of her feeding from me while they all watch makes my cock harden. I press it against her, and her eyes flare black.

"Drink from me now," I say and dip her. When I bring her back up, I plant a kiss on her lips. Her mouth moves over mine, slowly. Appreciatively.

The kiss is quick because Millie is the one who pulls away. I'd fuck her here in front of everyone if she'd let me.

"I don't know, Teddy."

I twist her around, her back to my front, allowing me to bring my wrist to her mouth.

The entire room seems to lean in. They're watching us. Everyone is staring our way with fangs bared or eyes glowing. It should scare me, but instead, I'm eager.

And extremely turned on.

Millie hesitantly wraps her fingers around my forearm and brings her lips to my flesh.

Otis continues to play, but the notes fade away and all I see and hear and *feel* is *her*.

My vampire queen.

I press my lips to her neck and whisper, "I'm yours."

She sinks her fangs into my wrist, and I groan at the brief sting of pain. My free hand slides over Millie's front, squeezing her breast and pinching her nipple.

She moans and clutches my arm tighter, growling as she draws my blood from the bite.

I don't care that all eyes are on us. My hand slips beneath the bottom of her dress, and I push aside her panties.

"So wet, my queen," I say before plunging two fingers inside her.

She bucks against me as I curl my fingers, grazing her g-spot. I start pumping in and out slowly because I know how much that frustrates her. When she moves her hips, signaling that she wants me to fuck her faster, I speed up my thrusts.

It doesn't take long to build Millie up to her release. Maybe it's because we're being watched. Or maybe it's my blood. A combination of both? Whatever the reason, the moment I press my thumb over her clit, she unlatches from my wrist to scream out as an orgasm washes over her.

I let her shakes subside before removing my fingers and shoving them into her mouth.

She licks them clean.

The room applauds, and I twist Millie back around to kiss her, tasting a combination of wine, blood, and her sweet pussy on her lips.

"Tell me why you think my blood is special," I say the moment we part. "And what that man said about me making the supes foam—"

She clamps her hand over my mouth, stopping me from speaking. Glancing around, I notice everyone has yet to look away. We *did* put on quite the show. Are they hoping for more? I move us closer to the stage and the loud music.

"Will this drown out our conversation?"

"Not really. Teddy, look. I'll tell you everything. But here is not the place. I just wanted tonight to be fun and special because I know how much you love music. I should have known better. There are too many supernatural beings here with enhanced hearing. They're a bunch of nosy fuckers who should be minding their own business, but

I'm a vampire queen with a human lover, and they want to know what makes you special."

I look to my left and spot an exit sign. I take Millie's hand and pull her toward the door. It leads us to a hallway and another door at the end, which opens to a trash area. Before the door shuts, I notice her bodyguards following. Millie holds up her hand and they stop before exiting with us.

"Will this do?"

She sniffs the air and listens for a few seconds.

"If we whisper, yes."

"Good," I say, then push her up against the wall. "Tell me everything while I fuck you."

"Teddy," she warns.

I unzip my jeans and pull out my cock.

"No, Millie. You've been keeping things from me."

I kick her legs apart and slip my hand underneath her short black dress again. This time, I have no patience and rip the thin material of her underwear off her body.

She gasps as my fingers slide into her wet cunt. My other hand wraps around her throat as I drive them in and out of her.

"This is your punishment. You don't get to come until you tell me."

"I already came."

"That was for them. This one's for me. You come when I say, okay?"

She nods and moans and grips the arm choking her. Her nails dig into my flesh until I bleed, and she swoops the blood up with her fingertip and pops it into her mouth.

God, that was hot.

"Can't. Talk," Millie wheezes.

"I didn't know you could breathe," I say, easing up but not releasing her neck just yet. I lean in to take her nipple into my mouth, tonguing it through the fabric of her dress.

She whimpers.

"I don't need air to survive, but I still breathe out of habit. But for speaking, I need my vocal box and you were crushing it."

I remove my fingers from her hair to wrap one of her legs around my waist, then I line my cock up to her opening.

"Fine, now talk."

I thrust into her, and she clamps a hand over her mouth to hold in her scream. She removes it once getting control of her pleasure.

"I... I believe... you might be... my blood mate," she whispers, the words broken as I fuck her against the wall.

I pause inside her to the hilt.

"What is a blood mate?" I mouth, making sure we can't be heard by anyone inside the club.

She squirms, trying to get me to move.

"Is that like a soulmate?" I ask, and she winces. "Of course. It all makes sense."

"What?"

"This connection between us. I mean, I've had one-night stands before but never any like this."

I pull out of Millie only to slam back in. Her eyes roll into the back of her head as I piston into her.

"Bite me again. All my blood is yours."

She shakes her head. "I took too much—"

"Take more."

I drop my hold from her throat so she can press her mouth against my neck. She scrapes her teeth over the skin. I moan, nearly coming as I pump into her faster, harder.

She's no longer holding in her screams.

"That's right Millie. Scream so everyone in this neighborhood and inside the club hears how well I fuck you. No more whispering, right?"

"Yes," she wails.

She's close and right before she comes, I stop. She fists my shirt and tries to move her hips, but I have her pinned to the wall.

I tease her with a soft kiss and lick a fang. Then I kiss her harder, allowing the sharp canine to pierce my bottom lip. She greedily drinks the blood that slowly pools out.

I start fucking her again.

"Feed from me, Millie."

"What if I can't stop?"

"You were able to stop when feeding from me on the dance floor. And you stopped right before I stabbed you earlier. I trust you."

She's already worked up enough that it takes a few more pumps for her to come.

Her fangs sink into my neck the moment her pussy walls choke my cock, and I'm sent over the edge with her. I wait until every last drop of cum is inside her before I withdraw. Millie stops drinking from me, refusing to take much of my blood this time.

"Now," I begin, tucking my dick back in my pants and zipping up. I help Millie smooth out her dress and fix her hair. "When we go back inside, every supernatural being will smell my cum dripping from your cunt and they'll see your bite on my neck. There will be no doubt who I belong to."

We move to walk inside, but Millie whips around and pushes me behind her. Her guards rush out, but she holds up a hand, stopping them from advancing.

"What the hell, Millie?"

"Quite unbecoming of a queen to fuck a human while feeding from them in public," a dark voice says.

A man appears from the shadows, holding up a delirious blonde woman in front of him. Blood drips from her neck and streaks down the front of her white dress. He clearly fed from her and didn't stop.

I gulp. "Is she..."

"Dead?" He tosses her to the ground as if she's a doll. "She will be soon."

He sniffs the air, which is something I've noticed a lot of supernatural beings doing tonight.

"This human of yours smells delectable, Mildred. Would you consider sharing him? Like old times?"

"Fuck you, Henry," Millie growls, and I've never heard her sound so... territorial. Not even with Layla.

Henry? Wait. I know that name. This is the vampire who turned her. Who made her do horrible things against her will.

He's slimmer than me, but still built. Taller too. Handsome in that mysterious and dangerous way. He has long black hair, which is tied up in a man bun. His eyes are silver, like Millie's, and I wonder if that's because he sired her.

"Ah. The ever so feisty, Mildred Maycot. The one who got away."

I want to kill this man. I want to drive a stake through his heart for everything he did to Millie. And now the poor woman on the ground, drained of blood. She can't be older than twenty-two. I want to check on her, but I'm also terrified. Millie is shielding me from him for a reason.

"Why are you here, Henry?"

He slowly paces the small space, his hands behind his back. Under the building's security light, he resembles a horror movie monster. His victim's blood is evident around his mouth and chin. He's wearing all black clothes, otherwise I'm sure I'd see his frontside covered in blood as well.

"Of all my fifteen hundred years of existence, I've never been to the Big Apple. Can you believe that? Initially, I wasn't interested in coming to this pompous country. But after you've traveled the world and seen it all, what's left than to cross the pond? I've now been here for ten years. I've visited many cities across the United States, but never New York City."

He pauses and smirks.

"Quite the metropolis you have here, *Queen* Mildred."

"It's Millie, and when you're in my territory, you'll address me as Your Majesty."

Henry scoffs.

"If I have my way, it won't be your territory much longer. And if I were you," he drags his eyes to me. "I'd keep that human close. It'd be a shame if he were to go...

missing. Or found dead, much like the other bodies that have been piling up these past few days."

"It's you, isn't it?"

Henry shrugs. "Guess the only way for you to find out is to catch me and kill me. See if the deaths stop then."

"You will be sentenced to the sun when we catch you."

"And why haven't you detained me now, Mildred?" He feigns a gasp. "Oh, that's right."

In a flash, he has me by the throat.

"I am faster and stronger than you. Now you decide... Will you chase me or save him?"

Millie's guards are now moving toward the feral vamp, but he's gone in a blink. My eyes struggle to follow the action and seconds later, pain rips through my stomach. I clutch it, then pull my hands away.

They're covered in blood.

"Millie?"

I collapse to the ground and fall into darkness.

Chapter 13 - Millie

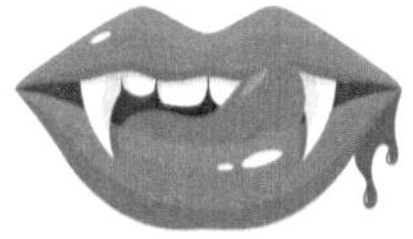

F uck, fuck, fuck.

My guards carry Teddy to the car and we're off, heading to an overnight clinic that treats humans attacked by supernatural beings.

I'm going to murder Henry.

I check Teddy's pulse and try not to freak out with how slow and weak it is. My hands are covered in his blood since I've been keeping pressure on the wound to slow the bleeding. Thankfully, it's not deep enough to have hit an organ, but he's still going to need a transfusion.

I curse myself for taking too much. Not just when I claimed him on that dance floor, and again when we fucked outside the club, but earlier at my penthouse.

He passed out for fuck's sake. But he begged me to drink from him. I was a fool.

You couldn't have known Henry would show up.

What the hell did he use to impale my mate?

My mate.

It's the first time I've truly let myself believe this human is meant to be with me.

It takes about ten minutes to arrive at SPN Emergency Services. It's discreet and disguised as a bodega to humans, but the medical clinic is in the back and spans three floors.

I had called ahead and told them to be ready.

"What do we got?" a wolf shifter asks upon meeting us at the door with a stretcher.

My griffin guards set him on top and the doctor gets to work.

"Stabbed by a vampire. He's lost a lot of blood tonight, because, um…"

The shifter holds up his wrist, then points at his neck. "Because you drank from him?"

"I *claimed* him at The 27 Club."

She raises a brown brow at me. "Twice?"

I shrug. "Wanted to be thorough."

She checks his pulse while a nurse hooks him up to an IV.

"It's weak. We need to get blood in him." She sniffs him, and her brown eyes glow yellow. "He smells different. Is that why you're drawn to him?"

"Or maybe I think he's hot and charming."

She snorts at my lie. It's not *really* a lie. Teddy *is* charming, *and* he's a beautiful man. He makes me laugh, feel appreciated, wanted. And while his blood is special, and he's likely my mate, I felt connected to him the moment I accidentally slammed a door in his face.

"What's his blood type?"

"AB."

"Negative?"

I nod.

"Interesting." She nods at the nurse who runs off to get a blood bag.

AB negative is a rare blood type. The moment I tasted him, I identified it. However, his blood type has nothing to do with why all the supes went crazy for him tonight. I mean, it didn't help having blood that isn't common. It's like a special treat for vamps.

If he's my blood mate, his blood would reflect that. I just don't know why or how, but it's the only explanation as to why everyone keeps saying he smells different.

There's just so much I don't know about this... bond? Destiny? *Fate.*

The nurse returns and hooks up a bag of O negative and they wheel him back into a room. I follow, taking Teddy's hand in mine.

Before the doctor can get to work on his wound, Teddy begins seizing. His body flails on the stretcher.

"He's rejecting the blood," the shifter yells, removing the line from his arm. She curses, palming her forehead. She looks at me, then back at him before returning her eyes to me. "Give him your blood."

"What? Why? You know it won't help—"

"I have a hunch." She doesn't let me question the request any longer and takes my arm to wipe it with an alcohol cloth. She finds a vein, stabs me with a needle, and connects the other end of the tube to Teddy's IV.

Within seconds of my blood entering his body, he stops seizing.

"That's what I thought," the shifter says. "The vampire queen has a blood mate."

T he wolf shifter, her name is Claudia I later learned, confirmed what I'd suspected after grabbing my best friend by the throat when she joked about killing Teddy.

I need answers. I want to know what to expect, especially since I'm no longer planning to face the sun—a decision that came too easily the moment Teddy's life was threatened by my sire. But also because Teddy being my blood mate will change everything. He gives me hope that I can love what I am.

I've put out a search for the two vampires who've experienced the blood mate bond and I'm awaiting their calls. Though it's an hour before sunrise and since they're extremely secretive and difficult to track down, it will likely be weeks until I hear from them.

I need to head home so I don't burn to a crisp under the sun's rays. Even once inside out of harm's way, and we stay awake when it's high in the sky, we become feverish. Our eyes, nose, and ears begin bleeding.

We were not created for the day, and we're punished when tempting the curse.

Ironic that death by sun is what I wanted just hours ago and now I'm rushing to avoid it.

Claudia says Teddy will sleep until sunset so my bodyguards load him up in the car and bring him back to a guest room in my penthouse. I'm worried about sleeping next to him. What if he wakes up after being nearly killed by a vampire and sees me and freaks out?

Teddy will also be starving when he wakes, and since I have no food or cookware at my penthouse, I send a text to one of my human assistants asking them to go to the store to pick everything up.

My sleep is restless. I toss and turn and dream about Teddy holding out his bloody hands, his face ashen, and his wavering voice as he said my name. I wake at sunset, not even sure how many hours of sleep I actually got, and head to the guest bedroom to check on him. But panic races through me when he's not there. I rush out into the living room and hear the clank of dishes in the kitchen.

"Hey! You're awake!" Teddy's cheerful voice greets me.

He smiles and gets back to work setting out his breakfast buffet.

"I woke up fucking starving and found all this food in your fridge. Man, I wish you could eat. I made pancakes, French toast, eggs, and sausage. It's going to taste so fucking good."

Oatmeal and an array of fresh fruit also crowd the kitchen table. He pours himself a cup of coffee and carries it to his place setting, adding to two other glasses of orange juice and apple juice.

He sits in front of his spread and digs in.

I gawk at him. "How... how are you..."

"Oh, I'm fucking fantastic!"

"No, I mean, how are you up and walking around after being stabbed over twelve hours ago?"

He takes a huge bite of pancake and shrugs. "No idea. I just know, I feel great. Kinda how I felt last night right after I licked your tears. My body is electrified almost. I can see clearer, this food?"

He stabs his pancake with his fork and tears off a chunk, then shoves it in his mouth.

He moans. *MOANS.*

"The flavors burst in my mouth, and it's like I can imagine the tree where the maple syrup was made from."

I walk to the table and grab his arm to stand him up. I lift his shirt and brush my fingers over his stomach.

No wound. Not even a scar.

Vampire blood can't do this. Our blood isn't a healing substance.

He giggles and folds away from my touch. "That tickles."

Wait. WAIT.

"Are you high?"

He sits back down and piles some eggs on his fork, devouring them in one bite. He waves the empty utensil at me.

"Perhaps."

Did my blood make him high?

"I need to make some calls."

"Alright, I'll be right here. You better come back so I can lay you out on this table and have you for dessert," he yells after me as I head to my room for my phone.

Layla is the first person I call.

"Hey! How's the puppy?"

I pace my bedroom. "He's high. Off my blood."

"Oh... that's not supposed to happen. Do you think that's a blood mate thing?"

"It has to be. Not to mention I was able to withstand a fae's magical current when it should have knocked me out cold. Any luck tracking down Elia and Noran so we can ask them about this?"

Layla sighs. "These vampires made it difficult to be found. They have no phone number or email on file. We have to send someone to their last known residences to deliver word that you are trying to get a hold of them, if they're even still there. We believe Elia and her mate are in Europe, Paris possibly, but Noran is said to be here in the states. Don't worry, we'll track them down eventually."

I pinch the bridge of my nose and close my eyes. I rarely stress and right now I am losing my mind not knowing what's happening with Teddy.

"Any updates on the search for Henry?"

"Nothing. The gargoyles are keeping a lookout. In the meantime, you should lay low."

"I will after the council meeting—"

"It's been canceled. They are up to date. We've also deployed soldiers to help track down Henry. We have it under control. You rest. Get to know your mate. Have lots of sex."

I laugh at my best friend who always knows how to talk me off a ledge.

"You should be on the throne, you know."

"Maybe one day."

That day will come sooner than she knows.

"I'll have extra guards stationed at your penthouse. Now that Henry knows about Teddy, I have no doubt he will try to find him and kill him."

I wince. "He was always a jealous prick."

He could have easily killed Teddy outside the club. Instead, I believe he only critically injured him to punish me.

I left him all those years ago after finding a witch to break his sire connection to me. Something that required black magic. The process was painful, as if my entire body had been engulfed in flames. It lasted for days.

Henry must have felt the same effects because he's been searching for me ever since.

I'm confused as to why he didn't capture me outside the club. To be fair, kidnapping a queen would be a dumb thing to do. Even he knows this.

Or maybe he doesn't want me at all. With Henry, anything is possible.

Still, he will not hesitate to take Teddy from me. I have no doubt he watched us fucking and heard us talking about Teddy being my blood mate.

Henry is a sadist. He won't want me to be happy.

I'll keep Teddy safe. Now, I just need to convince him to move in.

Chapter 14 - Teddy

It's been two weeks since I nearly died and Millie's blood saved me—something that shouldn't have worked but did. Millie had told me vampire blood doesn't cure injuries or illnesses. So why was I the exception? She says it's because I'm different. Special.

Her blood mate.

After growing up feeling as if I was insignificant, with parents who gave me more rules than love and affection, I found it hard to believe that I'm someone special.

I've never felt wanted before meeting Millie.

And now she's worried about Henry still being out there, killing humans and leaving new bodies every day. She said he could come for me, so she asked me to move in and quit my job. I've never had anyone be so... territorial over me. That night in the club, hearing her call me 'mine' was... erotic. Addictive.

I have no doubt she can keep protecting me from the vampire who sired her.

I didn't hesitate to accept her offer. Leaving behind my life was easier than I thought. I emailed my resignation to work, telling them I had to move back to Kansas for a family emergency. They didn't question me, and to be honest, I wasn't close enough with any of my coworkers for them to pry. They were too busy with their own lives to get wrapped up in mine, and my friends outside of work were more like drinking buddies who I only met up with every once in a while.

I didn't realize how lonely that sounded. How lonely of a life I've lived.

I rarely talk to my parents anymore. They disapprove of the life I've made for myself. They've grown further and further apart from me ever since college when they made it clear how much they disapproved of me drinking and partying. Now I see them maybe once a year, either for Thanksgiving or Christmas—never both. We'll call each other on birthdays. They even send me a card with a twenty-five-dollar gift card to a coffee shop.

When I learned I had an inoperable brain tumor, it was my chance to escape. With no one to tell, no one to console me, I accepted that my life was over. Then I met this woman who's made me question my entire existence. She's opened my eyes to what my life could really be like.

She can save me.

She hasn't agreed to turn me, but after two weeks of sex and cuddling and getting to know each other, how could she not?

My attraction to her should scare me. I never thought I could commit myself to one person, but the idea of forever with Millie is invigorating.

The blood mate bond is intensifying our connection. It's consuming. As much as my body is trying to convince me I'm in love with her, I know it's not true. But I can see myself falling in love with her over time.

We're enjoying exploring our desires together. She lets me take control, but some nights I'm begging her to dominate me.

Like right now. I'm splayed out like a starfish, my arms and legs tied to the four corners of her bed frame. A blindfold covers my eyes and Millie has a flogger in her hands.

"Such an obedient puppy," she says and slaps the flogger's falls over my chest. The leather strikes my nipples hard enough that I arch off the bed and moan. "You look so appetizing right now spread out like this for me."

My cock jumps at the menace in her voice. My body recognizes the threat and anticipates the punishment.

"Puppy likes that, doesn't he?"

The nickname has grown on me.

I've always had too much energy; a byproduct of my parents limiting the things I could do. No video games, no television or movies. No technology whatsoever. I had my records, my music—the one thing they didn't control. I at least expected them to ban so-called 'risqué' bands. But they didn't. My mom loved music. She's the one who bought me all my albums. Of course, my father destroyed them the first time I got wasted and was found naked in a stranger's front lawn and arrested for public indecency. I had to call them for bail money.

When I was a kid, and I'd go grocery shopping with my mom, I'd make friends with any stranger who walked by. I'm surprised I was never kidnapped with how trusting I was with strangers. I suppose our small town in Kansas was safe enough, but that was before I learned about the existence of supernatural beings.

My parents let me play by myself outside, but only if it was within our fenced-in backyard. My father at least built me a treehouse when I was five. I'd climb it and pretend I was a knight defending my castle.

The flogger slaps across my thighs.

"Focus! You should only be thinking of me."

The bed dips and Millie straddles my hips. She rubs her wet cunt over the length of my shaft. I suck in a sharp breath when she grabs my cock and lines it up to her opening.

"I'm going to ride you hard and bring you to the brink of orgasm," she says and sinks down. "Then I'll stop, refusing to move until you beg me to let you come."

I tug on the binds and groan.

"So vocal for me."

She starts bouncing and digs her nails into my chest. My skin breaks and the sting adds to my pleasure.

"I'm getting close!" I grunt.

Millie pauses, my dick inside her to the hilt. I try to buck my hips, but she tsks and wraps her fingers around my throat.

"Bad puppy," she whispers.

Seconds later, her tongue laps up the blood from her claw marks on my chest while her grip on my neck tightens, cutting off my air supply.

"Please," I wheeze.

When I'm moments from passing out, she lets go and lifts off me. The flogger slaps across my stomach, and I tense at the sudden pain.

"I'm going to bite you now, and it's not going to be on your neck or your wrist."

She moves between my spread-out legs and the flogger comes down on my left thigh, then the right, hard enough that I'm sure there will be welts tomorrow. I jerk at the burning sensation of the slap; the binds digging into my wrists.

"Fuck, Millie!"

Two more slaps of the flogger.

"Sorry, *Your Majesty.*"

"Much better, pup."

She grabs my dick and squeezes before fisting it up and down. Precum leaks out of the tip, and I start shaking from the edging.

"Would you like to come?"

"Please, Your Majesty."

She licks the bead of cum off the top, then continues to fist me.

Her hair brushes against my inner thigh, tickling my sensitive skin before her fangs scrape over the area.

Holy shit.

Is she going to bite me on the thigh? I suppose the femoral artery is there.

Pressure builds in my spine and my balls tighten closer to my body. Then she stops, and I let out a sob/whine combination.

Her fingers tighten around my shaft at the same time her tongue swipes over my aching balls. She sucks on them and drags her teeth over the delicate skin. It's too much. Too *good*.

She must know I'm about to burst. Her mouth returns to my thigh, and she bites down, causing my eyes to roll into the back of my head as I erupt into an orgasm. Ropes of cum shoot out my cock, all over Millie's hand and my stomach.

I scream out my pleasure, my body shaking.

And I pass out.

I wake up to the smell of bacon and toast. My stomach growls and I force myself to roll out of bed.

Muscles all over my body ache as I hobble into the bathroom to relieve myself. Millie's bite on my thigh has already nearly healed.

I can't believe I passed out. The sex was that good. The orgasm too intense.

When I make it to the kitchen, she's setting a plate on the table.

"I heard you stirring," she says with a smile.

Seeing her face light up... seeing her *happy*... is my favorite thing. She hasn't told me a whole lot about her life. I can't imagine all the experiences she's had over the five hundred years she's lived. I think she's keeping the stories to herself because she's ashamed of some of those experiences.

Telling her about myself was humbling. Aside from my parents' strict upbringing and my sexual awakening in college, I didn't do much else. I didn't travel because I had no money. Unless you count trips to the lake during the summer with my college friends. We'd swim for hours, get drunk, grill, and sleep before doing it all again the next day.

After college, I got a job in finance and moved to New York City. I lost touch with all my college friends and struggled to make new ones. I worked too many hours, and my only entertainment was going to bars with coworkers and bringing home random hookups.

I haven't lived, and I'm hoping Millie will be the one to show me what living can really be like.

"You know how to cook?"

She walks over and wraps her arms around me. I lean in to kiss her. She sighs against my mouth, and I try to deepen the kiss, but she pulls away.

"Did you forget I was human once? I had a family to take care of. I'd make them breakfast, lunch, and dinner. Desserts were my specialty, though. Puddings, trifles, pies…" She drags me over to a chair and sits me down. "Plus, after I was turned, I got a job as a baker for a lord in London."

She hands me a fork and pushes the plate toward me. It has scrambled eggs slathered in cheese with a side of maple sugar bacon and toast with jam.

"You worked? I wouldn't think vampires need to work."

"Not necessarily but for me, charming people for the things I wanted was the easy way out. And to avoid losing my mind of boredom, I worked. Of course, being nocturnal meant I had to use compulsion to assure working between sundown and sunrise wouldn't be an issue.

"I held every job imaginable. At least ones women were allowed to do. My first job was the baking position I mentioned. The lord employed a cook, so my sole focus was on pastries and other desserts, all which I baked overnight. I once cleaned a castle for royals in Denmark, my vampire speed allowing eight hours' worth of cleaning to be done in a fraction of the time while everyone was sleeping through the night. I was also a seamstress for a high society woman in Spain. She didn't care what hours I sewed, as long as I had her dresses done before the ball or the dinner or the play. And I was an au pair for a vampire family in Paris with two undead toddlers."

I choke on my sip of coffee. "There are child vampires?"

"Turning children is now illegal, but back then, vampires had few rules. Most humans under the age of sixteen who were turned had to be killed. They're harder to teach control. They left too many bodies to be discovered."

I shiver at the disturbing picture Millie paints and distract my thoughts with the food she made. I stab at the cheese covered eggs and groan at the first bite.

"Good?"

"Fantastic!"

She chuckles, and not that I'm counting, but I've now made her laugh at least two dozen times since meeting her. I'm counting her smiles too. I've managed to catch more of those.

"Tell me about your family," I say, taking advantage of this rare moment where she's sharing her life with me.

She sighs as her memories resurface.

"I was never meant to be an obedient housewife," she says and sits down across from me with a glass of wine. "But that was the life women were dealt back then. I always loved the arts. My dream was to learn an instrument and play on stage at a concert hall in London. Then my father arranged me to marry the son of a farmer in the town over in exchange for farmland. I was very lucky that my husband, George, was kind. I was sixteen, and he was twenty-one when we were forced to marry."

She pauses and frowns. I don't say a word, waiting until she's comfortable. I know how difficult it must be for her to return to this part of her life.

"I struggled to bear a child. I feared my impotence would anger George, but he was surprisingly supportive. Finally, at age twenty, I gave birth. Our son, George Junior. Then five years later, Mary. We had planned for more. I had many failed pregnancies after Mary. But George never pressured me. He never lashed out at me. Over time, I do believe he loved me as I did him. I became the dutiful wife and mother, forgetting all about my artistic dreams. Don't get me wrong, I loved my family with all my heart. I..."

Her voice catches and she looks away. I reach out for her hand, taking it in mine.

"Then Henry found us. He would have tortured them. He would have prolonged their deaths with agonizing pain. He gave me the choice. A quick death by my hands or a long one by his."

I squeeze her hand.

"I'm sorry, Millie."

"Yes, well, it was a long time ago, so..."

"Grief doesn't care about time. You are allowed to mourn them however long you need."

She releases my hand and points at my plate. I abide her silent order and continue eating.

"Four hundred and seventy years later, and I don't know if losing them has ever gotten easier. I never got to properly grieve them. Not right away, at least. When Henry turned me, he compelled me to forget them. I got my memories back after the sire bond was broken, but I wish I hadn't. I didn't want to remember that night and how I murdered my own family."

She pauses and looks down at her hands as she wrings them anxiously. I set my fork down, no longer hungry. My stomach aches for Millie's tortured past.

"Did Henry ever force you to..."

"Have sex with him?" She purses her lips. "Yes, but it wasn't often. He liked to fuck his victims before taking their lives. Sometimes after their heart stopped beating too. He manipulated me, using his sire bond to force me to do horrible things alongside him. I grew to love it. Not every death by my hand was his doing."

"You were—"

"Don't make excuses for me, Teddy. I deserve no sympathy or reprieve."

Her hands ball into fists on the tabletop.

"I was a monster, and I never paid for my sins. I convinced myself I no longer deserved to live because of the things I did."

I pause and curl my fingers around the edge of the table. "What?"

She finally shakes herself out of the daze and locks eyes with me.

"The night we met was going to be my last. I was going to face the sun at dawn."

Chapter 15 - Millie

It's done.

He knows.

I'm not sure how I expected him to react. Angry, sad, confused.

"Millie..."

"I've obviously changed my mind—"

Teddy stands and grabs me by the wrist to pull me up into his arms. He cups my face in his hands and kisses me. It's slow, deep, desperate.

He moves us, slowly, until my back hits the kitchen island, then he slides his hands around to cup my ass. He squeezes roughly, and I moan against his mouth. Without breaking our now frantic kiss, he lifts me up to sit me on the counter.

He rubs his palms along my back, my hips, my legs. Anywhere he can touch. My hands are in his hair, tugging the strands to add a little pain to this sudden... shot of lust.

When he pulls away from the kiss, his cheeks are flared red, and his breathing is labored.

"Teddy—"

"Shut up," he whispers, and I scoff. "Just... shut up and let me convince you to never have those thoughts again."

My face must soften because he holds up his hand.

"I know you said you changed your mind, but hearing you say you wanted to face the sun... I can't imagine a world without you in it, Milli Vanilli."

He steps closer between my legs and rubs his palms over my thighs again.

"This is me begging you to let me worship you. Let me care for you and treat you like the queen you are. Let's spend the rest of our lives getting to know each other and fall in love."

I open my mouth, but he holds his finger over my lips. I'm tempted to bite that finger. I don't think anyone's ever shushed me before.

"I've already asked you to turn me. I know you don't want to..."

I do though.

I'm just terrified that I'll fall in love and lose him like I did my family. Or that we'd spend eternity together and he'll end up hating me and abandon me and I'll end up alone.

It's the same fear I have with Layla; that someday she'll grow tired of my company.

"I still have time to convince you. I mean, not a whole lot of time. The doctors did only give me like four months to live. And my body will begin shutting down at some point. I'll lose a lot of motor skills and—"

I clutch him by the shirt and tug him to me.

"Okay, I get it. I'll—"

"Think about it," Teddy finishes for me.

Why am I struggling with this so much? I turn him, and he lives. I don't, he dies, and I'll never see him again. I would have no reason to live if he's not in my life.

Aside from Layla, but she doesn't need me standing in her way any longer.

Maybe I'm fighting turning him because I'm enjoying human Teddy too much. Because every newborn vampire is different from the human life they once lived. They are more prone to blood lust and have to learn to control those urges.

Henry never did that for me. He encouraged my urges. Once I severed his hold over me, I called on a vampire friend to help rehab me. Someone who was killed by Henry once he found out all his hard work making me an 'evil vamp' had gone to waste.

I had already moved to America when I learned my friend was dead. I've lost too many people close to me, and I think that's my biggest hesitation.

"I see that head of yours working in overdrive so let's fix that."

Teddy pushes me down until I'm lying on the countertop. He tugs off my pants and underwear and teases my entrance with his fingertip.

"Mmm. So wet, Millie."

My fangs drop, and I close my eyes as he dips a finger in. He curls the tip, and I scream when it grazes my g-spot.

"I'm going to taste you now, Your Majesty."

Ugh, why do I love it so much when he calls me that?

I'm pretty sure he started doing it as a joke. Now I would beg him to call me that if he ever stopped.

Which is crazy since I do *not* want to be queen anymore.

I will always be his queen.

His lips descend on my clit, and he takes it in his mouth, lapping his tongue over the sensitive bundle of nerves. I move my hands to my breasts to play with my nipples and he adds a second finger.

He thrusts in deep, hitting that perfect spot, causing me to moan and arch off the countertop.

"That's what I want to hear from my queen."

My queen.

"Please," I whimper.

"Would you like to come?"

I nod, but he must have seen my nonverbal response because he drives his fingers into me harder while covering my clit with his mouth again. He reaches his free arm up and I grab him by the wrist. The moment my fangs sink in, my orgasm erupts.

Teddy waits until my pussy stops spasming before removing his fingers and licking them clean.

"Now, you'll never want to face the sun again. Isn't that right, Millie?"

"That's right, Puppy," I say and sit up to kiss him.

I taste myself on his lips and groan. I taste so sweet. It must be from the blood mate bond.

That's another reason I'm hesitant to turn him.

Does he realize how connected we would be? More so than the sire/fledgling bond? Would I have control over him like Henry had over me?

We need to talk about this but before I can utter a word, my phone rings. I curse against Teddy's lips and break the kiss to jump off the counter and grab my phone on the table.

"What?" I growl into the receiver.

"Wow, I must have caught you mid-fuck," Layla chuckles.

"What do you want?"

I make my way into my office, half naked, and thinking about all the ways I can torture my bestie for the interruption.

Layla, however, is unaffected by my attitude and sighs heavily.

"We have another body."

I curse. "That makes nearly two dozen now. The media will take notice soon, if they haven't already. We can't keep covering this up. Anything from the gargoyles?"

"No. They've managed to get glimpses of Henry but by the time they follow him, he's long gone."

That's because he's fifteen hundred years old. Even if we capture Henry, he's stronger, faster. He could take out dozens of vampires on his own in a battle.

But I'm determined to end him.

I *will* kill him.

Somehow.

"We need to draw him out," Layla says.

"And how do you suggest we do that?"

The other line is silent and if I didn't hear my friend's nervous tapping on whatever surface she's nearby, then I'd have thought she hung up.

"You won't like it."

"Say it and I'll decide if you should live or die over the suggestion."

She snorts, not even a little intimidated by my threat.

Because she knows I wouldn't hurt her.

Even if she hurt Teddy?

I shake the thought because my best friend would never lay a finger on my mate. She fights and kills those who deserve it, like her husband and the vampire who turned her... and the hunters who aim to destroy our kind. But she's never taken an innocent life. Even when she was a newborn vamp, she never let her urges win. She's always been so strong willed, which is why she deserves to be the Vampire Queen of New York City.

"We use Teddy as bait."

Or I kill her and find a new successor.

Chapter 16 - Teddy

"**A**bsolutely fucking not!"

Millie's been screaming at whoever's on the phone for the past five minutes. She hid away in her office, but the walls are no match for my queen's wrath. When she finally emerges, her fangs are out, and she has murder on her face. The killer emotion fades when she spots me.

"I'm afraid I have some royal business to attend to."

She's changed as well, now dressed in a red blouse and black pencil skirt. Her black hair is up in a high ponytail. Her makeup is light and natural and flawless.

She embodies every aspect of a queen as she walks to where I stand with her head held high. I grab her by the waist, and she relaxes slightly, draping her arms over my shoulders. She tries to kiss me, but I pull back.

"Tell me what's wrong."

She scrunches her nose and snarls her lip, simultaneously appearing adorable and fierce, before looking away.

"It's... nothing."

I chuckle. "Did you know when you lie, you can't make eye contact? You fidget too. And your voice goes up ever so slightly."

She rolls her eyes.

"Yeah, well, I only struggle lying to *you*. I'm an excellent liar when necessary. And when I don't feel like lying, I use compulsion. Which is another issue with you not being able to be hypnotized."

I smile at her using the word I love saying when describing compulsion. I do it to antagonize her because I love seeing her pissed off.... Because she ends up taking it out on me in the bedroom.

But my smile drops, and I stare her down, raising a brow, until she relents with a sigh. The silent treatment always works when she's trying to avoid speaking about something.

I rarely use the move, but I've learned over the past two weeks that Millie has never shared the details of her vampire life with anyone other than Layla. Getting 'personal' as she likes to call it, makes her uncomfortable. Sometimes

I sense she *wants* to talk but just needs my patience and encouragement.

"There's been another body," she says, slipping out of my hold.

I close my eyes and curse.

"I need to meet with the council tonight so we can go over a plan of capture. We've employed the gargoyles, who stand guard over this city, but they've had no luck. We've asked other vampires and supernatural beings to be on the lookout, but Henry is powerful. He's feared. No one will risk death to turn him in. If he's been spotted, nobody is saying a word."

"How could anyone be afraid of a man named Henry?"

Millie snorts. Not exactly the laugh I was hoping for, but I know she's stressed. She steps away to walk into the kitchen where she pours herself a glass of wine.

"Henry is what I called him because it pissed him off. Heinrich de la Nova is the cold-blooded killer who has murdered not only humans, but vampires alike. He has no remorse. He kills for fun, and he is starved for power."

I comb my hand through my hair, then scrub it down my face. "How do you plan to catch him? It sounds impossible."

She winces. Another sign that she wants to lie to me. Or that she regrets something she's done or is about to say.

"I need to figure out what he wants. If it's me, then I will draw him out. The council will have to approve a security team. Plant snipers on rooftops—"

"He can die by a bullet?"

"A wooden one, yes."

"What if he captures you?"

"Then I'll escape. I've outsmarted him once. I can do it again."

"How did you escape him?"

"He became bored of me," she begins, sipping her wine and resting a hip on the kitchen island. "He'd disappear for days, weeks. During one of these hiatuses, I sought a witch to break his sire hold over me. Then I packed up the few belongings to my name and left. I didn't imagine he'd care, but after a few months, I got word he was searching for me. I boarded a boat to America as soon as I could. He hated the new settlement. I knew it'd be the last place he'd come looking for me. I asked acquaintances to spread rumors of spotting me in various countries in Europe and the Middle East. Even Asia. It kept him busy."

And likely infuriated him.

"Then he finally finds you and sees you with a human."

She sets her glass down and returns to where I stand. She wraps her arms around my torso and leans her head on my chest. I cocoon her in my own arms, kissing the top of her head.

"Stabbing you was a warning. He was letting me know that he's still in control, even after all these years with the sire bond broken."

"Use me."

She lifts her head. "What?"

"Let me be bait."

"Did you hear my conversation with Layla?"

"No. Did she suggest the same thing? Then it sounds like—"

"It's not going to happen. *I* need to be the one to face Henry. *I* can draw him out. He will not get anywhere near you."

"What if he kills you?"

She peels herself out of my arms and turns her back to me. "And, what? You lose your ticket to immortality?"

My heart drops.

"Is that what you think I care about?"

"Is it not? It's what you want."

"Of course it is!"

She turns at my raised voice, shock riddling her face. I never raise my voice.

"I don't want to die, and I don't want to leave you."

My eyes burn and my throat aches with unshed tears.

She reaches out for me, but I step back.

"I want to spend the rest of my life loving you. I know it's too soon for both of us to say we're in love, but isn't the chance that we could fall in love worth exploring? Isn't it worth living for?"

A tear falls down my cheek and I wipe it away.

Millie says nothing, letting me get everything out.

"I want you to turn me for you, not just for me. Because you deserve love too. You lived all these years thinking you're a monster, but a monster wouldn't feel remorse for the lives it's taken. A monster wouldn't feel compassion. And a monster wouldn't put their life on the line to protect someone else.

"But turn me because you want this too. Make me a vampire so you will no longer be alone. I don't want you to ever feel as if you don't deserve to be happy."

She's crying now too and seeing the lines of red against her pale skin reminds me of winter... a rose in the snow. My cold-skinned queen who turns my body into flames with how much I desire her.

She's mentioned the lack of a soul, but I don't believe it. How could I feel such a connection to an empty shell? She's more than this monster she claims to be.

If she's cursed, then I'll gladly be damned with her.

She wipes the blood off her cheeks, and I grab her by the wrist, taking her soiled fingers into my mouth and sucking them clean.

I cup her cheek and graze my thumb over her lips. My touch draws out her fangs, and I press the pad of my thumb over the point until piercing a hole in my skin. I shove the bleeding tip into her mouth. Her tongue flicks over the wound.

When I remove the digit, I spin Millie around and fold her over the top of the kitchen table.

She grunts at the unexpected action, which I find amusing that my slow human speed surprised her.

"Teddy," she warns. "You're insatiable. You just laid me out on top of the counter and made me come."

I smooth my hand up her spine, then back down to grab the hem of her pencil skirt. I roll the fabric up over her hips, revealing her plump bare ass because she's wearing a thong. My hand crashes down and she arches away from the table.

"And now I'm going to fuck you on the table."

"Layla will be here soon," she groans.

I take my cock out of my sweats and pull the thong to the side.

"Then you better come fast."

I slide into her with one hard thrust and she screams, clutching the edge of the table while I ream into her from behind.

"You feel so good, Millie. Your cunt was made for me. Only me."

I use the bunched-up material of her pencil skirt like the horn of a saddle and drive into her.

"No one else will ever feel this pussy clench again. No one else will ever get to *taste* you again. Only me."

With my free hand, I strike her ass cheeks, one after the other, at least a dozen times on each side.

"Fuck, Teddy," she wails.

She may be a vampire... any wound she receives heals within minutes... but she can still feel pain.

She loves it. My lashes turn her on, and her pussy walls tighten, letting me know she's getting closer to orgasm.

Millie's cellphone rings. Layla is here.

"What did I say, Millie?"

I clutch her long hair and wrap it around my wrist, tugging her head back. She whimpers.

"Come. Fast."

"That's right, Your Majesty."

That does it.

She erupts with her release. Her body shakes and her cunt milks my cock, sending me over the edge as well.

I rest my head on her back as I try to catch my breath. But I barely have time to recuperate before Layla is pounding on the door.

"Five minutes," Millie says to Layla. She doesn't even need to raise her voice because she knows her friend will be able to hear her.

I'm reluctant to let my queen go, especially since she wants to use herself as bait to capture her ex. But I stand and slowly remove myself from her.

"Wait," I say before allowing her to get up.

I watch as my cum leaks out and I lap some of it up with two fingers. Then I walk around the table to where Millie's head rests and clutch her ponytail to tug her head back. I shove my fingers in her mouth, and she moans around them but dutifully licks them clean.

"That's my girl."

Layla pounds on the door again, likely annoyed for having to wait.

"Stand." I help her off the table, then grip her by the chin. "I would clean you up, but I want you dripping with my release while addressing the council, letting them smell me on you. Because you're mine."

She whimpers at my words, struggling to sheath her fangs. Her eyes are still black as well.

My hot as fuck vampy babe.

I kneel to adjust her skirt, rolling it back down and smoothing it out while Millie fixes her blouse. She'll need to redo her ponytail and touch up her makeup.

The thought of me causing this disheveled appearance makes me smile as I look up at her from where I kneel.

Her palm covers my cheek.

"I like seeing you on your knees before me." She moves her hand up to my forehead to push back my hair. "I'll petition the council tonight to approve your turning."

I stand and wrap my arm around her waist to bring her flush with my body.

"Really?"

"The only sun I need is you."

"Ugh," Layla says, deciding she's tired of waiting and lets herself in. "Could you two be any more disgustingly sweet?"

"We could," I say and grin.

Layla rolls her eyes but smiles. I've noticed she's rarely angry like me. She might try to put on the scary grumpy vampire act sometimes, but I can see past that mask.

"I'm afraid I have to steal your mate away," Layla says to me.

Millie sighs and brings me in for one more kiss.

"I will have guards stationed outside the penthouse door and around the building. Do not go anywhere while I'm away."

"Yes, ma'am."

She narrows her eyes at me. "You'll pay for that."

Maybe I should call her ma'am more often.

"Looking forward to it, *ma'am*."

Chapter 17 - Millie

The drive to Lower Manhattan from Midtown will take about twenty minutes. My mind races with what I'm going to say to the council. I've never requested to turn someone before. Vampires who have been undead for over two hundred years are allowed to sire a human. If that fledgling perishes, they can request another—as long as they're not requesting to sire more than one human every one hundred years.

It's not that vampires hate being alone. We're sexual, and we want companionship, but on our terms... no commitment. Sometimes vampires sire because they're bored and want a pet, or someone they can order around and mentor. Newbie vampires have to be taught control, learn discipline. Otherwise they'd kill freely, and the human population would dwindle.

Most vampires in royal positions come into the role with their fledgling. Or they find a human to turn soon after. No one questioned why I didn't have one, but they all knew. I've made it clear over the years that I didn't want to be responsible for bringing another person into this life.

Or maybe I was waiting for my mate.

Before the rules were implemented that vampires had to gain permission to sire a human, the majority were done without consent. Now the human has to provide verbal permission. Tonight I'll present my case and once Henry is killed, I will bring Teddy to appear before the council where he'll publicly grant me permission.

"You haven't chewed on your nails in decades," Layla says, and I jump at her voice. She chuckles. "And I've definitely never seen you startle."

"I'm stressed. Leave me alone."

She grabs me by the wrist and pulls my hand away from my mouth.

"Talk to me."

She weaves her fingers with mine and I let out a shaky breath. My friend is so patient with me. She can read my moods better than anyone.

Aside, now, from Teddy.

"Remember when we used to talk for hours until dawn?" she begins, sensing my hesitation to share my concerns. "We'd get drunk off boozed blood and gush about our crushes?"

"I do not gush nor have crushes."

"You're right. You're very selective when it comes to your partners." She squeezes my hand and I glance her way. A bright smile lights up her beautiful face. If Teddy is my golden retriever sun, then my best friend is the moon who guides me at night.

I've been an asshole by not telling her what I had planned. She deserves to know.

I turn in my seat to face her. "I need to confess."

Layla slips her hand from mine because she knows when I lower my voice to a serious tone that I'm about to drop a bomb.

"I had planned to face the sun the night I met Teddy."

"What?"

Layla's fangs drop. She never lets them drop. Yep. She's pissed.

"Why? Why would you—"

Her voice cracks, and she turns away.

"Fuck you, Millie, for making me cry. You know I don't like to get my face bloody."

"I'm sorry. Obviously, I've changed my mind, but you have to understand... I tortured myself for the things I've done. The innocent lives I took. I convinced myself the world would be better without me. I was miserable, bored, and lonely. Of course, I had you, but I was holding you back from great things—"

"The hell you were!"

"Layla, please. You had given me companionship, and I knew I would never get that type of friendship again. You deserve more than being my advisor."

"And you thought ending your life would have, what? Released me?"

"Yes."

"That's absurd, Millie May."

"I know. I realize that now. I didn't want to bother you with my depressive thoughts, and I sought an easy way out."

She scoffs. "But then you met Teddy, and he's your blood mate. Your chance at true love. Is that the only reason you changed your mind?"

"*He* is the reason, blood mate or not."

"Was I not enough for you to stay?"

"You will always be enough, but I was blinded by my horrible past. Teddy helped me realize that I'm not the monster I convinced myself to be."

"I could have convinced you of that if you had just talked to me."

"I know. I'm sorry. I'm an idiot."

Layla sighs, her tense demeanor softening. "You *are* an idiot, but Millie, I'm here for you. I will always be here for you. Anytime you want to talk. Or if you need to see someone else... a professional..."

I take her hand again and squeeze it once. "Thank you, but trust me, I'll never have those thoughts again."

Layla nods and turns her head to stare out the window. The silence between us lasts for an agonizing two minutes. I know it was that long because I anxiously counted in my head.

She huffs. "So what now? You turn Teddy and live happily ever after as Vampire Queen of New York City and her fledgling prince consort?"

"Yes and no. Yes, we will live happily ever after, learning to love each other. But I will no longer be queen."

"I don't understand."

"I want you to have my crown. At least, that is what I will tell the council once I abdicate."

"Millie, you can't."

"I can and I will. You have always been a better fit for the role. You help me make decisions. You have lived longer than me and you are wiser—"

"I highly doubt that."

"And you want this more than I do."

She purses her lips and crosses her arms, thinking about my words.

"If you don't want it—"

"I do."

"Good. Then once Henry is taken care of and Teddy is turned, I will relinquish the throne."

We don't speak the rest of the drive, and I'm sure it's because Layla is in shock... or she's attempting to accept my proposal to hand over the righteous title.

We pull up to WOVE Council Hall within five minutes. My security team surrounds us walking in, not taking chances with Henry lingering in the shadows somewhere in the city.

The council hall is inside one of New York City's oldest buildings with drab marble floors and boring brown and tan walls. Artwork of old, important vampires hang on the wall—including an oil painting of me from when I was first named queen.

The meeting takes place in a large room with a circular table that reminds me of a secret society or a team of villains meeting to plan world domination.

The council is already seated when I enter. The main purpose of this advisory body is to create, maintain, and enforce the rules of our kind. There are ten vampires in total and every member is older than me. Ten voices, with mine being the deciding factor.

It's too much pressure. Too much responsibility. I like control, but not when it's deciding important outcomes of other people's lives. I never wanted this role but felt I had a duty to fulfill it.

Everything is about to change.

I approach the table and stand to address the group.

"Thank you for joining me for this emergency meeting. As you all know, Heinrich de la Nova is the vampire responsible for the many human deaths across our city over the past two weeks. He has escaped capture, and we can no longer allow this rampant killer to remain loose and threaten our existence."

The men and women around the room nod in agreement.

"My plan is simple, and it will not be up for discussion."

Everyone leans forward because this is the first time I've refused their council. I am allowed to do so as queen, but I never felt a need to override their decisions.

"Heinrich is my sire. Therefore, it is my responsibility to end him. I will be the one to draw him out."

Raised voices fill the room as the council adamantly renounces this plan. I hold up my hand and they hush.

"As I said, this plan is final. I'll visit the summer night market in Bryant Park. It's no secret that it's one of my frequent haunts. If Heinrich is tracking my whereabouts, he'll follow me there.

"I will need an undercover team ready with stakes and guns... snipers on rooftops. I'll wear a stake-proof vest as well."

Angry and disagreeing voices raise up again.

"I know he is stronger and faster, but if we get him out in the open, then I can wound him or distract him while the team moves in. They can deploy sunlight chains to capture him."

WOVE researchers created the UV infused metal a few years back to help vampire soldiers take down FVs in a more efficient way. It's still in testing phases, but it's the one thing that will keep Henry down while I stake him in the heart.

"And if you die?" a vampire named Heidi asks. She's a petite blonde from Sweden who was turned at age eighteen but has lived eight hundred years since.

"Then I have my replacement written in my will."

More head shaking and grumbles reverberate through the room.

"When will this plan of yours happen?" a vamp named Zeke asks. He's a svelte man from Ghana who was turned at age thirty over six hundred years ago.

"Tomorrow night—"

"Why wait that long when the gang's all here?"

We all turn toward Henry's voice as he enters through the double doors dragging Teddy by the neck.

This means the guards I stationed outside my penthouse are either dead or critically injured.

"You son of a bitch!" I yell and start toward him.

He clutches Teddy's neck tighter.

"Ah ah, Queen. I won't hesitate to kill him."

Teddy's eyes are drooping. He's pissed himself, and he's deathly pale.

Henry drank from him.

"You've been hiding this tasty human all for yourself, Mildred. And he cannot be compelled? How strange indeed."

"Let him go and take me instead."

Henry tsks.

"If I do that, then I have nothing to use as leverage to get what I want."

"And what might that be?"

"For one?"

In a blur—even for my enhanced eyes—Henry releases Teddy to speed around the room, staking every guard flanking the walls. One by one, the ten men and women burst into flames. Henry's back in place, catching Teddy before he hits the ground.

"There. Now they can't try to kill me."

The guards outside the door to this room are also likely dead. I glance up to my two griffins, Wylan and Merc, perched in the rafters where they keep watch anytime I'm in this room. I shake my head, letting them know to wait for my order.

Henry should know that backup is on the way.

Unless he already killed them too.

Why did I think we could defeat him? In a flash, he took out the security in one of the most highly protected rooms. He's gone mad with power, and he will kill anything that gets in his way.

The council members cower in their chairs, all refusing to stand up to Henry. Even those who are nearly as old as him.

They don't want to fight. They don't know *how* to fight. And they definitely don't want to die.

"Second, I'd like to take control of this council. Not as king, but as your God."

I scoff, and Henry punishes my reaction by stabbing Teddy in the stomach with the dagger he's been holding at his side.

It takes everything in me not to rush to my mate.

"It's time for our kind to stop hiding and emerge from the shadows," he says, addressing the room. "I know there are other supernatural beings who share this belief. We should be working together to overpower the human race and rightfully take our spot at the top of the food chain. As vampires, we should be *farming* the humans. They are our food, not our friends."

He locks eyes with me.

"And certainly not our lovers."

"If you think we will allow this—" a council member begins, but she's abruptly cut off when Henry lets go of Teddy once again to blur across the room and punch his fist in her chest, pulling out her heart. Teddy is back in his hold before the thousand-year-old vamp collapses to the floor.

"Anyone else in disagreement?"

He waits, but no one says a word.

"Not even you, Mildred?"

"Give me Teddy, and I'll voice my thoughts in return."

Henry smiles, and I cringe at how handsome he appears. He's always been handsome, but that never negated from the pure evil coursing through his veins.

"Sure." Henry shrugs. "You can have him back."

He slits Teddy's throat before tossing his body toward me.

Chapter 18 - Teddy

My ears ring.

I drown in pain.

My vision blurs.

I'm dying.

I collapse to the floor, vaguely aware of the fighting next to me.

How am I still alive?

I can *feel* my blood gushing out of the wound on my neck. My heartbeat is slowing. My body relaxes as life drains from me.

But I stay.

I watch.

Millie launches herself at Henry. He stabs her in the stomach, just like he had done to me.

She doesn't back down. She latches her arm around his neck and uses her weight to bring him to the ground. He wasn't expecting the move, and they land with Millie underneath him—her front to his back. She wraps her legs around his waist.

"Now, Layla," she screams, though the words sound muffled, as if I'm underwater.

I struggle to keep my eyes open, but I have to see.

Layla stands over Henry, a stake in her hands, and she brings it down. The wood sinks down into his chest. The last thing I remember before passing out is his body bursting into flames.

"**S**tay with me," a familiar voice says.

Millie?

"Yes, Teddy, it's me. I need you to drink."

My mouth is full of blood, and I'm not sure if it's mine or Millie's.

"Please. You will die if you do not drink."

Die? I was already going to die. But I still had a few months left. I don't want to die now. It's too soon.

Wait. Is this… is this really happening? Is Millie turning me? I weakly clasp her arm and start drinking.

Angry voices reach my ears, muffled like my vision is blurred.

Millie's blood isn't healing me this time. I'm pretty sure I'm in some weird limbo between life and death. I'm unnaturally cold and as hard as I try, I can't feel my heartbeat. Am I dead?

"Yes," Millie answers, even though I'm not saying the words out loud. "My blood brought you back, but it's not enough this time. You must complete the turn to survive."

"You do not have the right to do this," someone says.

"He's my blood mate."

"What? Impossible."

"You heard Henry. His blood is unusual. He can't be compelled. Those are signs of a blood mate. *My* blood mate. I've claimed him."

"It's true. She's highly protective of him too," Layla adds. "And they've been inseparable since meeting two weeks ago. You know vampires never get that territorial or attached to a human, even the ones they intend to sire."

"I love him," Millie says with a sob.

A chorus of gasps fill the room.

"Please, I can't let him die. I won't be able to live without him. I will face the sun if he…"

Her words trail. Bloody tears fall down Millie's face as she combs her fingers through my hair while I feed from her.

"He has to consent."

All heads in the room turn to me. I give them a weak thumbs up since I can't speak. The informal motion of permission garners some chuckles, including a tearful laugh from my queen.

"The rules state he must verbally consent," an older man with salt and pepper hair begins. "But very well. It's clear this is a unique case. We will have more thorough questioning for you and your fledgling after his turn. Are we clear, Your Majesty?"

"Yes," Millie says, not once looking away from me as I ingest her blood.

"I will send for a donor. He will need one to complete the turn."

The room starts to clear, and a man is sent in a few minutes later.

"You've had enough, Teddy."

I don't want to stop. Millie's blood is too good. But the moment the man approaches us, I *smell* it.

I smell *him*.

His human blood.

I release Millie's arm and sit up, clutching my throat. It burns with how much I want this man's blood.

"This is Ayame," Millie says, and he sits on the ground next to us.

He's a beautiful man. Tall and thick with dark brown skin and rich brown eyes.

"He has given consent for you to feed from him," Millie continues. "I'll puncture his skin since you don't have fangs yet. You'll get those once the transformation begins. It'll take a few days and it's going to be extremely painful. Do you understand, Teddy?"

"Yes."

It's all I can say because I'm both terrified and *excited*.

Millie leans in and bites Ayame on the neck. Once she moves back, he repositions himself to straddle me.

Oh. Wow. This is intimate.

"Feeding *is* intimate."

I didn't realize I had said that out loud.

"But he's straddling you so you can easily drink from him."

Millie places a palm on my shoulder.

"I'll be right here watching."

Fuck. Why is that hot?

If I weren't in between life and death, maybe this turning ceremony could be something entirely different.

"Clear your mind, Teddy. Those thoughts are not very helpful right now."

You can hear my thoughts?!

"Yes. Now drink so you're not wasting Ayame's blood."

My mouth covers the bite wound, and I draw the thick, warm liquid past my lips.

I groan and wrap my arms around the man. He gasps, but not in fear. I can taste his pleasure.

"Easy, Teddy," Millie whispers.

I drink from Ayame for only a few minutes before Millie stops me.

I could have kept feeding.

"His heart was beginning to slow. You have enough of my blood and his for the transformation to be successful."

Millie holds out her hands to help me and Ayame stand. She turns to him.

"Thank you for your donation."

He nods and leaves us, and I briefly wonder if Millie got his phone number so we can revisit my earlier thoughts.

"He'll be easy to track down," she says with a small chuckle, once again reading my thoughts. I should ask her about that, but I'm starting to feel woozy. "We should go. We have an hour before sunrise."

Millie walks us out of the room, and she passes me off to two guards who nearly carry me because of how delirious I am.

I feel drunk and high and out of my body.

I don't remember much after that. Only pain that seems to last for days upon end.

Searing pain as if my blood has been set on fire.

Biting pain as if ice water has been thrown on the flames encasing my body.

Piercing pain as if I'm being stabbed over every inch of my skin.

Feverish pain as if I've become ill with a virus that's making me sweat and toss and turn.

Aching pain within my mouth as my fangs grow.

And finally, a gasping pain as life leaves my body.

The transformation is complete.

Chapter 19 - Millie

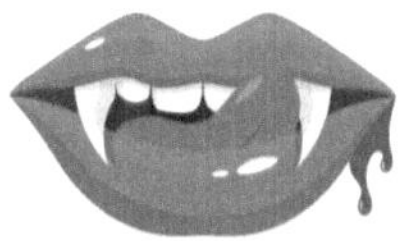

It's been four whole days and Teddy still hasn't woken up.

I stand at the end of my bed, arms crossed, staring at him... willing him to be okay.

What if something's wrong? What if I was too late?

"You know there's a saying, 'a watched pot never boils,'" Layla says, standing at the door of my room.

"He should be awake by now. Fledglings only need a full day's sleep after the transformation."

"Yes, but he's a blood mate. He's... magical." Layla flashes her hands and wiggles her fingers.

I groan. "If only we knew more about that *magic*."

I drop my arms and leave since I can't telepathically will my sleeping beauty to wake.

"That's actually why I'm here," Layla says, following me as I shut the bedroom door and walk down the hallway. "Noran has arrived."

"What? Now? It's two hours until sunrise. And why the hell didn't you lead with that?!"

In a millisecond, I'm in the living room where Noran stands at my bookcase, admiring my art and memorabilia collection.

He selects a book and turns, holding it up.

"A Shakespeare first edition," he says, smiling. He opens the book to the first page. "And it's signed with a personal message. 'To Mildred, thank you for convincing me not to name my character after you. There can only be one Mildred in my life.'"

Noran is a slim man, with icy blue eyes and bleach blond hair pulled back into a low ponytail. His cheeks are sunken in, and his skin is sickly pale. He looks as if he will break at the slightest touch.

He's impeccably dressed, a fitted black suit and shirt with a skinny red tie.

"Yes, well, Mildred Capulet doesn't have the same ring, now does it?"

I met William when I was newly turned. Less than one hundred years a vampire. Henry had taken me to a performance of *The Taming of the Shrew* and after the show, he disappeared with one of the actors. I loved the play so much, I tracked down Shakespeare himself to offer my accolades... and to make him my next meal. I considered killing him after taking his blood, but his talent was too good to let his life end.

We had a week's long affair instead.

Noran chuckles. "I suppose you're right."

He puts the book back on the shelf.

"Please, have a seat. Would you like something to drink?"

"Wine is fine."

Noran and I sit in the armchairs while Layla grabs us drinks. The future queen of New York City shouldn't be waiting on us, but she knows how eager I am to talk to this vampire.

"I hear you've found your blood mate."

"I have. And where might yours be?"

Noran raises a brow at me. "He's not in this city, which is full of blood thirsty supernaturals."

Layla returns with our drinks. Noran takes his glass and casually sips on the bitter liquid.

"Your mate will always be desired by other supernaturals. His blood is infused with... something ethereal. We just don't know what that ethereal component is exactly or much about why someone is destined to be a vampire's mate. Does he have a rare blood type?"

I nod.

"Then he was likely born with this... fate, but the older he got and the closer to meeting his match, the more potent the magic became. Was he ill when you met?"

I suck in a breath, eyes wide. "Inoperable brain tumor."

"Yes. That was the result of his body slowly fading; the magic feeding off his soul to survive. My mate had become ill with a neurological disease. He was unable to be compelled as well."

Just like Teddy.

"Sounds more like a parasite," Layla mumbles.

Noran chuckles. "Yes, well, if a blood mate is the product of witches, then I have no doubt it is a curse in its own right."

"Tell me everything. Teddy has been sleeping for four days since I turned him."

Noran takes a sip of his wine to compose his thoughts.

"He should be waking soon. His body is preparing him for the bond."

"The bond?"

"You have to complete the blood mate bond."

I must have a confused look on my face because Noran waves his hand around.

"It's simple. You fuck. You come together. You drink from each other."

"Sounds similar to how the gargoyles accept their fated mate bond," Layla snorts.

"The witches are responsible for the curse on the gargoyles as well," Noran says. "They are either clever or lazy with their spell casting."

I nod blankly, tapping my fingertips on my lips as I try to narrow down all the questions I have.

"Are the rumors true about what happens after we've mated?"

"Yes. It's all true. Your heart will beat once again. Your tears will be real. You'll be able to take a midday stroll. You can love. *True* love. Your soul will be restored."

I almost cry thinking about it.

"But it has its limitations. While your heart beats, it will be slow. One or two beats per minute. Therefore, you are still not technically alive. Don't tempt this gift. You can withstand sunlight but too much will still make you sick. You and your mate will fall madly in love, but he's in control of that connection. He will be capable of breaking the bond if he ever so chooses. Though I doubt that would happen. Blood mates are extremely loyal. It would take an act of God to break that connection."

We will fall madly in love.

I repeat Noran's words in my head.

I told the council I loved Teddy. Vampires never say the word. But I did, even though Teddy and I are not yet fully bonded.

Am I already in love with him?

I knew love when I was human, but what I have for Teddy feels different. I'm eager to spend the rest of our lives exploring it.

"If he's in control of our connection, does that mean I won't be able to control him like most sires are able to do?"

"That is correct. The bond will not allow it."

That's a relief. Not that I would have tried to control Teddy, but it's good to know that my sire abilities won't work with him.

"The downside of having a blood mate is the fact that he will be a walking blood bag."

"Even now that he's a vampire?"

"More so. His blood is extremely desirable. He can be drained, and while it won't kill him, it *will* be painful. It happened once to my mate. I suggest befriending a witch and having a protection spell placed on him."

Witches work with supernatural beings all the time, even vampires. They no longer hate us. Well, not all of them. The elders still aren't our fans, and the United Witch Authority refuses to break the vampire curse.

They made us evil then have the audacity to get mad when we do evil things yet refuse to put an end to it?

I suppose it's also likely that the witches who cursed us used dark magic and assured there wouldn't be a way to reverse our curse.

Noran glances at his watch and stands. "I must be going, but do not hesitate to call if you have any other questions."

He slips his hand into his suit jacket pocket, extracts a card, and hands it to me.

"So, you do have a phone number?"

He chuckles. "Yes, but only a handful of people have it. Don't abuse it, Queen."

"I won't. Thank you," I say. "I'm sure I'll be speaking with you soon."

The moment Noran is out the door, something barrels into me.

Teddy.

He has me pinned to the wall by the throat, fangs bared.

"Layla, leave," Teddy growls, locking eyes with me. "I need to fuck my mate."

I watch Layla walk to the kitchen island and grab her purse.

"Don't have to tell me twice," she says and zooms out of the penthouse, leaving me alone with my newly turned—and apparently extremely horny—fledgling.

"How long have you been awake?" I ask, my voice strained because of the pressure he's putting on my neck.

"Enough to hear *everything* that man said."

Teddy sniffs, then inhales deeper. The pupils of his green eyes—now infused with specks of gold—expand and his face lights up with *hunger*.

"Fuck, Millie, I can smell how turned on you are. Should I squeeze your throat harder?"

He doesn't wait for my answer and puts more pressure in all the right places.

I whimper and the sound sets him off.

He tears off my clothes... *literally.* They're in shreds on the floor. He drops his pants and removes his shirt next. He grabs my leg to hook it around his waist and while he has me pinned to the wall, he slams into me.

I scream and he moans and picks up the pace, realizing he now has vampire strength.

I hold on to his shoulders as he pistons his hips. His mouth crashes against mine, claiming my lips with rough kisses. Since he's not used to the fangs, the sharp canines scrape and puncture my lips and tongue. The wounds leak blood, which fills his mouth. He growls, *possessively.*

I'm impressed with how he's able to control this new-found strength as he squeezes my neck harder. Any other fledgling would have crushed muscles, ligaments, and more by now.

He's putting the *perfect* amount of pressure on my throat.

He slips his free hand between us until finding my clit, massaging it lightly at first then pressing harder.

That's what sends me over the edge.

He fucks me through my orgasm, then once my pussy stops contracting, he slips out of me and pushes me down to my knees.

I immediately open my mouth and he shoves his cock inside.

"You're going to swallow all my cum, Millie."

"Mhm," I hum around his length.

He slides in and out, the tip hitting the back of my throat, causing him to moan. He grabs a chunk of my hair to hold my head in place and starts fucking my mouth just as hard as he was fucking my cunt minutes ago.

Human Teddy loved to have control, but he held back. Vampire Teddy has no mercy.

And I am absolutely here for it.

I reach around him to squeeze his ass cheeks. He groans and pumps faster. When I swallow around him, he explodes. Webs of cum shoot down my throat, and I take every last drop like a good girl.

When he pulls out, he sits on the floor next to me. A goofy smile spreads across his face. I'm glad the turn hasn't taken that part of this man away from me.

"We didn't bond," I say, taking his hand and weaving my fingers with his.

"I know. I just really needed to fuck you."

I laugh and rest my head on his shoulder.

"You didn't think we were done, did you?" Teddy asks.

"Umm... no?"

He clutches my jaw so he can look at me.

"That was just round one."

Chapter 20 - Teddy

I've never felt so *alive.*

I stand and hold out my hand. Millie doesn't hesitate taking it.

"How are you feeling?" she asks as I lead her to the bedroom.

Our bedroom.

"It's as if an electrified wire has replaced my veins. Everything is sharper. Colors more vibrant. Wait..."

I pause in the hallway and listen.

"I can hear people in this building talking and the cars driving on the street. Incredible."

We're in the penthouse of a sixty-floor high-rise. My enhanced senses are overwhelming but exciting all the same.

"You'll learn to filter those sounds out and focus on what you want to hear. But I was talking about your hunger."

I push Millie up against the wall. "I'm definitely hungry."

I kiss her and she whimpers when my fangs cut into her lips again—something else I'll have to get used to.

She breaks off the kiss, but I can't get enough of her and trail my lips across her jaw and down to her neck.

"I was talking about your need for blood, Puppy."

Mmm. I've been transformed into a cold-blooded killer, and she still calls me puppy. I love it.

"What should I be feeling? Because the only part of me that is in need of satisfying is my cock. It needs to be back inside you."

She giggles and it quickly turns into a moan when I scrape my fangs over her skin. I'm already getting hard despite emptying everything down Millie's throat minutes ago.

"Most fledglings are ravenous when they wake up from the turn. They need to feed immediately. In fact, they struggle not to kill any human in their path. This building is full of beating hearts."

My fangs cut her neck deep enough for small drops of blood to surface. I lap it all up.

"You're all I need… right now and forever."

She sinks her fingers in my hair and latches on, pulling my head back.

"I'm serious, Teddy. I need you to tell me if you need to feed. I'm talking about human blood, not me," she adds before I can joke. "You will get stomach pangs, your fangs will ache, and your throat will feel as if you've swallowed hot coals."

"Don't you worry, my queen. I'll tell you when I'm ready for blood."

She rolls her eyes but smiles.

"Now will you let me fuck you so we can complete our blood mate bond?"

She nods, her smile stretching wider, lighting up her beautiful face.

I take her hand and lead her to the bed. We're still naked from our quickie in the living room so I spin her around and push her onto the mattress. Her tits bounce and belly jiggles in the most delectable way.

She moves to the middle of the bed.

"I need to ask you about hearing my thoughts," I say, crawling up her body. "That wasn't a hallucination while I was dying, right? You can hear what I'm thinking?"

I place soft kisses along her legs and thighs.

"Yes," she sighs when I reach her pussy and huff a breath on her slickness. "You should be able to hear mine too. You'll have to learn how to open your mind to it."

I continue up her stomach to her breasts where I take a nipple into my mouth and suck. She arches off the bed.

I release it with a pop. "Is that normal or a blood mate thing?"

Her other nipple is in my mouth before she can answer, and I scrape my teeth over it. She screams and bucks.

"Blood mate," she says, the words hampered by her lust. I pause to let her continue. "I think. I forgot to ask Noran, but it has to be. Henry could never hear my thoughts."

"Tell me how you and Layla killed him," I say and return my attention to her breasts.

"He expected me to fight—oh fuck, Teddy," she moans as I scrape my fangs across her nipple again. Not bad. Maybe it won't take long for me to get the hang of them. Despite my desperate urge to fuck her right now, I stop my pleasurable torture so I can hear the rest of how badass my mate is. "He didn't expect Layla to fight though. So I distracted him with a headlock and took him down to the ground which allowed Layla to stake him. I honestly didn't think it'd be that easy. It's satisfying because Henry never liked to be outshone, especially by a woman."

"And it was sexy as fuck," I say and without warning, I plunge my fangs into the peak of Millie's breast.

She screams, her back bowing at the sensation. Her blood pours into my mouth while I lash my tongue over her sensitive nipple. I slide my hand down her stomach, finding her soaked cunt and slipping two fingers inside.

I pump in and out and bring her to the cusp of orgasm. Then stop. I unlatch my mouth and remove my fingers.

"No!" she whines.

I use my newfound speed to readjust us on the bed, sitting with my back to the headboard and Millie straddling me.

"Are you ready?"

"More than ever."

She grabs my cock, lines it up to her entrance, and sinks down. She throws her head back in a moan, and I grunt at how *tight* she is for me.

With her hands clutching my shoulders for leverage, she rides me. Her sharp nails dig into my skin but I barely register the pain.

"I'm already close, Millie," I huff.

"Me too."

My palms slide to her back, and I skim them up then down until cupping her thick ass and squeezing.

We cling to each other as if trying to morph our bodies into one. The more of our skin that touches, the quicker I get to orgasm.

As if her skin is hot-wired straight to my cock.

"Now, Teddy. Bite me now."

I bury my face into the crook of her neck and pierce her skin. Her blood fills my mouth and gushes down my throat, causing me to erupt with pleasure. Millie mirrors my actions. Her fangs impale my neck with greediness, and she growls—something she does often when feeding from me.

Her pussy walls milk me dry of cum, spasming around my dick for what feels like hours.

Once we've both had enough blood—somehow knowing when to stop—we retract our fangs and just sit there, cocooned in each other's arms.

"That was..." I begin, struggling to find the right word.

"Euphoric?"

"Exhilarating."

"Intoxicating."

"Mind-blowing."

Millie laughs. "All the words. It was all of them."

"Do you feel different? Noran said you'd be able to withstand the sun."

She reaches up to move a piece of sweaty hair off my forehead.

"That's something else I need to ask Noran: How long after we bond before I change?"

I glance out her UV protected windows and see the sky brightening.

"I'll call him later tonight," she says, following my gaze. "Right now? I want to cuddle with you and fall asleep."

"I've been sleeping for days."

"Then maybe I need to wear you out with more sex."

In a blur, I take us into the bathroom, my cock still inside Millie and her legs wrapped tight around my waist. I grow hard, ready to take her up on that offer.

"Deal," I say. "Let's start in the shower."

And I slam her against the tile.

Epilogue - Millie
Four Weeks Later

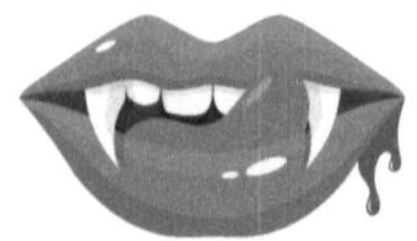

L ayla's coronation is tonight.

It's been four weeks of blood mate honeymoon bliss. Teddy and I spent the entire time in bed, giving ourselves to each other. Then we emerged from our sex dungeon because it was time to begin the process of naming Layla as my successor.

The council wasn't surprised by my abdication. Most were shocked it took this long. Layla had been calling the shots for the past month anyway and before that, she was my closest advisor who I frequently consulted for decisions when it came to the throne.

She's going to be fantastic.

Teddy walks out of our massive walk-in closet in a black suit, black dress shirt, and a sleek red tie to match my off the shoulders, tea-length dress.

It has pockets too!

"Your Majesty," he says, coming up behind me while I do my final checks in the mirror.

"You won't be able to call me that anymore here in a couple of hours."

He wraps his arms around my waist and gently kisses my neck.

"You will always be my queen."

I turn around and drape my arms over his shoulders. With my heels, we're closer to the same height.

"You can always go back to calling me Milli Vanilli. You know I've always loved that nickname."

He gives me a soft kiss, knowing not to mess up my lipstick.

"Only if you go back to calling me Theodore. My full name on your lips is sexy as fuck."

One night after we fucked and went into hours' long pillow talk, Teddy told me about his parents calling him Theodore. How he hated the name until I claimed it, erased the history attached to it, and made it into a term of endearment.

I snort. "We've only known each other for two months. We have forever to think of all the cute nicknames for each other."

Without a word, he pulls me into the living room, leaving me in the middle to search through my record collection.

After a few seconds, he finds one and puts it on the player.

You're My Latest, My Greatest Inspiration by Teddy Pendergrass starts playing.

Teddy returns to me, taking my hand and sliding his other around my waist.

Not that I'm counting, but this is the twentieth time Teddy has danced with me in the living room.

But I'm not counting.

"It's the twenty-first actually," Teddy says, responding to my thoughts.

He's been working on opening his mind to me. We've also learned more about our newfound connection.

We invited Noran and his mate over for dinner that first week after we bonded.

Noran's partner, Sione, is twice his size and a sunshine man just like my puppy. They met when Noran was traveling the world after becoming bored with his life... just as I had. He ventured to Samoa and Sione saved him. Well,

Sione thought he was saving a human from drowning in the ocean, but Noran was floating in the water, waiting to be consumed by the sunrise.

Their story is similar to mine and Teddy's. Teddy saved me, and he's the only sun I need.

Except, now I can withstand the sun's rays. Noran says the change in my body was immediate. After they left, Teddy and I watched the sunrise together. Because he is my blood mate, he can do everything I can: face the sun without bursting to flames, crying real tears not bloody ones, and hearing my thoughts—which Noran says is necessary when we're out in public so we can communicate silently if facing a threat.

We've yet to go out in public since we've bonded, but I've already hired plenty of security to keep us protected.

"One hundred," Teddy says, pulling me from my thoughts.

"What?"

"One hundred. That's how many times you've smiled since we met."

I smile again and look away. Teddy clutches my chin so he can lock eyes with me.

His beautiful green and gold eyes.

"One hundred and one."

Another smile from me.

"One hundred and two."

"Okay, okay!" I laugh. "Why are you so adorable?"

"Is it because you love me?"

"Maybe."

He dips me and I giggle.

"Fine! Yes! I love you."

"Good because I love you and it would have been awkward if you didn't love me back. Especially since we're blood mates and immortal and living together. Do vampires get married? Because I vow to never leave you. Sorry not sorry. You're stuck with me."

My stomach flutters at his words.

"You're obsessed."

"So are you."

My phone rings.

"Your Majesty," I say, answering Layla's call.

"Are you on the way?"

"We're about to leave."

"Ugh, can you hurry. I'm freaking out."

"Why?"

I can hear her pacing.

"Because I'm about to be named Vampire Queen of New York City and it's something I've been dreaming about forever and now it's happening. Also, I just found out that the council wants to test supernaturals working together."

"We already work together."

"When necessary, yes, but they want more unification. They want a gargoyle to lead my security team."

"What? Why?"

She sighs. I know she's twisting her hair into knots as we speak.

Her nervous tick.

And it takes a lot to make a vampire nervous.

"They said once supernaturals interact and cohabitate with no issues—and you know how stubborn and territorial supes are—then the closer we are to revealing ourselves to the world. They want to prevent another Henry incident. Trying to control the human race will only lead to war, so the plan is to gain the trust of humans in powerful positions first, convince them we are not a danger, then reveal ourselves to the world as a united front."

Interesting. I never imagined a day when the human world and supernaturals would coexist.

"Sounds like a good idea to me."

She huffs into the phone.

"Whatever. Can you just get here? I need my best friend."

I glance at Teddy, and he raises a brow, hearing every word Layla has said.

"Leaving now."

I say goodbye to the future queen and turn to walk back to Teddy.

"Did I tell you how sexy you look tonight?"

I hold up my finger. "Behave your thoughts, Puppy. Layla will stake us on sight if we're late."

He shrugs. "Guess I'll just have to fuck you in the car."

I open my mouth to argue but clamp it shut.

"Good idea. Let's go."

And with that, Teddy takes my hand and I lead him out of the penthouse.

The moment we're in the elevator, Teddy says, "I'm really glad you hit me with that door."

"It was an accident, and you know it."

"Are you sure?"

"Yes."

"Well, you're wrong." He wags his eyebrows at me, letting me know he's up to no good.

"Am I?"

"Yes, because the night we met, my friends and I were walking to a different bar. We got lost and ended up on the street where minutes later, I'm being attacked by a door."

"Not attacked."

"So, you see, it wasn't an accident. It was fate. We were destined to meet. You were always meant to hit me with that door."

Something drew him there to me, and I'm confident it was the blood mate bond.

He was destined to be my sunshine.

My reason to live.

The End

Thank You

Did you enjoy A Vow for the Vamp? Please consider leaving a review on Amazon, Goodreads, or StoryGraph. Or please share on your social media! Don't be afraid to slide into my DMs (as long as you're not mean)!

Want more monsters? Check out Gaga for the Gargoyle and Guardians for the Vamp. Locheran and Farrah's book, Giddy for the Gargoyle is out now. Get it on Amazon!

Acknowledgements

Let me tell you why this one was special. 2024 was a rough year for me. At the end of March, I had a hysterectomy. There were complications and because of that, my recovery took longer. Then I had a second surgery at the end of June to fix an issue that arose during those complications. I wrote this entire book on my phone while in bed recovering from those two surgeries.

If you're wondering why I wrote the FMC as the vampire and not the man? Well, it's because we need more vampy babe stories! And, more plus-size vampires! I mean, come on! Fat vamps are a thing! Because vampires are real, right? RIGHT? But, yeah, I wanted to portray a fat vampire who wasn't ashamed to be immortalized in a big body. Millie may have hated being a vampire because of the horrible things she did, but she never hated her body.

I want to thank my beta readers: Xan Garcia, Gina Hejtmanek, Mikaelynn Rose, Suzi Vee, and Kara Robinson. I loved all your reactions you left in the Google doc! And your critiques were more than helpful.

Thank you to my editor Jenny Sliger with Owl Eyes Proofs & Edits. You will always be my comma defender.

To my cover artist: Wavyhues. I love how you depicted my characters, especially Millie and her beautiful, big body.

And to the readers who have been with me from the beginning and to the ones who just found me, to the readers who buy my books no matter what I release, to the readers who constantly like my posts and share them... I love you all. You mean the world to me and you are the reason I keep writing!

Also by Settle Myer

Guardians for the Vamp

A Manhattan Monsters Romance

FFM with a Vampire/Sphinx/Gargoyle

The monsters of Manhattan are tired of living in the shadows. The new vampire queen, Layla, is tasked to come up with an unveiling plan, but she finds herself distracted by her new broody gargoyle guard... and the bossy sphinx on the unveiling committee. Find it on Amazon & KU.

Gaga for the Gargoyle

A Fated Mates Monster Romance.

Gaga for the Gargoyle is about 999-year-old gargoyle king, Xander, who has 6 months to find his fated mate before permanently turning to stone. Enter a strange dating app that pairs him with Evangeline, a 40-year-old human. This book is part of the Fated Dates series, a shared world about plus-size MCs meeting their monster mates through a mysterious dating app. Find it on Amazon & KU

A Vow for the Vamp

A Manhattan Monsters Romance.

500-year-old vampire queen, Millie, is ready to face the sun, no longer able to live with the guilt of the monster she's become. When she goes out for one last feed, she meets a 29-year-old golden retriever man named Teddy... who just might be the reason she lives. It's on Amazon & KU

Deadly Deceit & Deadly Obsession

Mafia Romance (New York City Syndicate Book 1 & 2) Deadly Deceit is the first book and Deadly Obsession is book 2. Both are standalones. They are dark cozy romance meaning the romance is sweet... but the story includes dark themes. Find them on Amazon & KU

The Off Script Series

Beyond the Bright Lights is the first book in the Off Script series of spicy standalone contemporary romances. It features Lana & Mylan's story. Beyond the Fame is book two and features Rebecca & Jensen's story. Beyond the Spotlight is the third and final book and features Savannah & Reynold's story. Find them on Amazon & KU. Beyond the Bright Lights & Beyond the Fame are on Audible

The Trinity Trilogy

If you love action & adventure, badass women with superpowers, diverse characters, found family, and fated mates—check out my sci-fi romance trilogy. Book 1 is a sweet romance with some cursing and violence, but books 2 & 3 have a sprinkle of spice in them. Trinity Found, Trinity Returns, Trinity Rises. Find them on Amazonand Audible.

Social Media

Check out my website and sign up for my newsletter for updates on new books, discounts, and sneak peeks!

https://www.settlemyerauthor.com/

Join my readers group. Become a Settle Myer Star and be a part of the discussion with other fans. I also posts fun facts about my books, characters, and more!

Follow me on social media

tiktok.com/@settlemyerauthor

instagram.com/settlemyerauthor

facebook.com/settlemyerauthor

About the Author

Settle Myer lives in New York City with her cats Zombie, Michonne & Birdie. She's currently a TV news writer who hopes to one day leave a world of death, disaster, and politics to write about worlds with plenty of cinnamon roll men and badass women. She loves all things zombies, cats, karaoke, and tattoos... but not necessarily in that order.